Weak Daze at a Public School

Reimagining Approaches to Mental and Behavioral Health

AHMAD KERSEY

ISBN: 979-8-9951256-0-0

Reimagining Approaches to Mental and Behavioral Health

"A man who views the world the same at 50 as he did at 20 has wasted 30 years of his life." Muhammad Ali

We are facing a mental healthcare crisis in this country, marked by rising rates of psychotropic medication prescriptions, suicides, mental health breakdowns, and related incidents. For example, according to the CDC, suicide rates have increased by 30% in the United States over the past two decades, even as the availability of mental health resources and trained professionals has grown. Prescriptions for antidepressants and other psychotropic medications have similarly reached record highs. Why, then, are these issues escalating? Are we missing something in how we address mental health crises? Is it possible that our strategies, though well-intentioned, are not as effective as we had hoped? In this piece, I will examine why our current approaches may be falling short and propose new strategies for meaningful change.

As you read on, I invite you to consider the following: Are we overlooking foundational factors in our mental health systems? Is the DSM-5 outdated, and do therapists and clinicians need retraining to meet today's challenges? What changes should we implement to better support families, clients, and students? If more resources alone aren't solving the problem, what fundamental shifts are needed in our approach to mental health? Reflect on how these circumstances developed, what happened before each crisis, and how many years of unaddressed trauma does it take before a person reaches their breaking point?

As healthcare professionals, we play a crucial role in ensuring that patient care is grounded in honesty and understanding. Living in truth means recognizing and communicating facts clearly, both about ourselves and the people we serve. For example, before diagnosing or treating a patient, consider whether they can fully comprehend your explanations—some may struggle with reading or understanding medical terminology. Adjust your approach by using plain language, visual aids, or interpreters when needed. To genuinely help others, it's essential to reflect on your own experiences and honestly assess how they may influence your approach to patient care. Testing your skills and ideologies involves regularly evaluating how you communicate, interpret symptoms, and make decisions. Practical steps to improve include: learning about your patients' cultural backgrounds and health beliefs, seeking feedback from colleagues on your communication style and clinical reasoning, and consciously examining your own biases. By taking these actions, you can provide more effective, empathetic care. Remember, self-improvement is ongoing—embrace opportunities to learn, adapt, and grow. Prioritize your own well-being so you can better serve others, and don't hesitate to ask for help or resources when needed.

"The dots of your life never connect until you look back."
Robert Herjavec, Shark Tank

Dedications

Thank you to my grandparents, Vivian Conley, Reginald “Gene” and Mary Kersey. Vivian explained and instilled the importance of education and “made” me go to Howard University. Sadly, after finishing my first year, I didn’t make it home in time to talk to her. My last time seeing her alive was in a hospital bed. Gene raised me and came out of retirement from Delco Battery, went back to work and paid my rent in Washington D.C. for that year. Fast forward through all the years of wandering, depression, working, and partying, I found myself homeless. Mary opened her doors and allowed me to get on my feet. Mary supported me when I had my first child. I needed her to survive, graduate, and move forward with my life. She escorted me on my graduation day from Ball State University.

To the village, Muncie, Indiana, that raised me. The church. My family (Kersey, Shaw, Hill, Conley, Robertson, Evans, Casey, Young, Edwards, Rankin, Williams, Barnes, Shabazz, Anderson, Jones, Stevens, Long, Davis, Rivers). The teachers, faculty, staff, and students at Howard University, Ball State University, Ivy Tech, Charles W. Fairbanks IPS 105, Avondale Meadows Academy, and Herron High School. Thanks for your dedication and hard work.

Forward

The inspiration behind the book started with watching the deterioration of the public school system. Children in public schools read at a lower rate than those in private or charter schools, but not by much. The numeracy rate of American children is equally alarming. I've spent countless hours in the classroom, staring at confused students who have lost hope in learning. An ineffective curriculum constrains teachers. The continuous public criticism of how their students perform on standardized tests is unfair. Even when strategies are proven not to work, teachers must follow protocol to keep their jobs. Sight words replace phonics, confusing, time-consuming processes, substitute math facts. An ineffective curriculum stifles brilliant children, lacks student advancement strategies or protocols, and frustrates, under-resources, and exhausts teachers.

Quick story: While sitting in a classroom supporting a student, I observed a brilliant, advanced first grader wandering around, looking for toys and books to play with. (To stay HIPAA compliant, let's call him "J".) He should have been sitting in the circle with the rest of the students, as his teacher was reading to the class. I stated, "Hey, boy. What are you doing? You're supposed to be over there, sitting with your class, reading."

As he continued to play, he replied, "That stuff is for babies. I already know all that."

To prove him wrong, I said, "Show me you can read, and I'll leave you alone."

He calmly walked over to the group, snatched a book from another boy's hand, walked over to me, and started reading. He finished that book in less than 2 minutes. He threw the book back to the boy and walked over to the bookshelf. "You want to see me ready another one? All this stuff is too easy." He grabs another book and starts reading aloud, disrupting the teacher and the other students. "Mr. Ahmad, 'J', is supposed to be over here reading with us, but he never can sit still. He's in trouble with me every day. I call the office and let them deal with it. I'm going to put in a referral for services to see you. I think he has ADHD."

Very calmly, I asked, "Can he just get another book to read? That's all he asked for."

"No. District says he's supposed to be in circle time. He can't read books on his own." She replied.

To make a long story even longer, the teacher referred J for services. After an unofficial assessment,

I found myself in a dilemma. Would I follow protocol for skills training and therapeutic interventions, or try something different? Because I knew where this referral stemmed from, I chose the latter. I conducted a test while waiting for the official intake process to begin. I called to schedule the intake. Reaching an agreement with his parents and the 3rd-grade teachers, I asked to bring a student into their classes to "observe" the behavior of older kids during my scheduled breaks, and they agreed. Once in the class, he received assignments and books from that grade. "J" never got out of his seat, had any negative behaviors, and was fully engaged in his schoolwork.

I knew it! I was onto something. This strategy continued for a couple of weeks, until his teacher inquired about the time he had spent away from her class. Once my plan was discovered and foiled, J returned to his classroom and displayed aggressive negative behaviors. He was more difficult to control than ever before. Later in the year, his parents wanted to move him to another school. Before he left, I reminded J of how intelligent he was. I told his parents that he was special and that he needed to find a school where he could thrive.

- Did I make any mistakes? If so, name them and give alternative strategies to use.
- Should I have trained/coached him to behave in the first-grade class?
- What other approaches could be taken?
- How much responsibility does the school district hold for having a plan for students like these?
- Should literacy pretesting be mandatory for entry to public schools? What about vision and hearing testing?

We need solutions for our students.

Challenge your country, province, state, city, county, or township to address these issues.

Healthcare is comprehensive.

Weak Daze at a Public School

By Ahmad Kersey

CONTENTS

Prologue and Analysis by Dr. Calvin Spinks, LPC, NCC, BC-TMH

Dr. Cal Spinks, LPC, NCC, BC-TMH, is a seasoned behavioral health clinician, counselor educator, and founder of *Quantum* and the *Second Genesis Foundation.* With over 30 years of experience in the mental health field and 16 years as a counselor educator, He has worked at Northwestern University, Concordia University, and Walden University. Dr. Spinks has built a career at the intersection of healing, education, and community empowerment.

He brings a trauma-informed, culturally responsive approach to his work, integrating clinical expertise with deep personal insight. His practice centers on individuals navigating stress, life transitions, identity development, and burnout, with a strong commitment to serving BIPOC, LGBTQ+, veterans, and helping professionals. Whether in the therapy room, the classroom, or the boardroom, Dr. Spinks fosters spaces where people feel seen, supported, and equipped to move toward clarity and sustainable well-being.

In 2016, Dr. Spinks founded *Quantum Consulting Group*, a behavioral health and consulting group committed to transforming care and leadership through culturally grounded, liberation-focused practices. Quantum serves individuals, organizations, and systems with a focus on integrity, alignment, and long-term impact.

As part of his broader mission to advance mental health equity, he also leads the *Second Genesis Foundation*, a nonprofit organization dedicated to providing accessible, high-quality mental health services to underserved and marginalized communities. Through direct services, education, and community-based initiatives, Second Genesis expands access to healing and builds capacity within historically overlooked communities.

Across all his roles, Dr. Spinks remains dedicated to developing ethical, socially conscious clinicians and creating pathways to collective and personal transformation. His work is rooted in the belief that wellness is not just the absence of distress, but the presence of connection, purpose, and possibility.

What This Book Is, at Its Core

Weak Daze at a Public School is a **collection of interconnected fictionalized case narratives** set in an under-resourced urban public elementary school. The stories function as **composite vignettes** rather than a traditional linear novel.

The author's stated purpose is threefold:

1. Humanize the lived experiences of children in poverty.

2. Expose how trauma, neglect, systems failure, and culture collide in schools.
3. Provide discussion prompts for educators, clinicians, and trainees.

The tone is intentionally raw, informal, and vernacular. The book positions itself as **pedagogical fiction** rather than literature for entertainment.

Structural Overview

The book is organized into **four major story arcs**, each with multiple chapters and shared characters. Each arc ends with:

- "Did you know" sections citing public health or education research.
- Discussion questions framed for classroom or training use.

Recurring Setting

- A predominantly Black and Brown public school.
- High poverty.
- Understaffed.
- Heavy reliance on informal supports.
- Strong presence of community figures (bus drivers, social workers, church staff).

Core Narrative Arcs and What They Cover

1. The Attack of the Killer Weave

Primary focus: Identity, body image, peer influence, adult neglect, and cultural messaging.

What happens:

- A group of elementary-aged girls navigates peer pressure around appearance, particularly hair and "adultified" beauty standards.
- A weave becomes a literal and symbolic device that alters behavior, confidence, and social dynamics.
- The weave "possesses" multiple girls, escalating behavior problems, sexualized conduct, aggression, and school consequences.
- Adults respond inconsistently, often punitively.
- The arc ends with a moral lesson about natural identity, health risks of synthetic hair, and self-worth.

What the story is really about:

- Early sexualization.
- Adultification bias.
- Internalized misogyny.
- Parental absence and exhaustion.
- How material culture becomes scaffolding for children's identity.

Arc 1: *The Attack of the Killer Weave*

Core Clinical Issues

- Adultification bias.
- Early sexualization.
- Identity formation under racialized beauty standards.
- Behavioral escalation as attachment-seeking and peer regulation.
- Somatic and symbolic control over self-image.

Clinical Risks if Unframed

- Reinforcement of stereotypes about Black girls' sexuality.
- Pathologizing normative identity experimentation.
- Misreading behavior as deviance instead of a stress response.
- Reader fixation on "problem behavior" rather than environmental contributors.

Clinical Recommendations

1. **Explicitly frame behavior as adaptive, not pathological.**
   Emphasize that attention-seeking, imitation, and peer alignment are developmentally typical and are intensified by stress and adult absence.
2. **Name adultification bias directly.**
   Clinicians and educators should be prompted

   to examine how adult interpretations accelerate punishment.
3. **Shift focuses from the object to the system.** The weave is a symbol, not the cause. Clinically, the intervention target is:
    - Supervision gaps.
    - Media saturation.
    - Caregiver fatigue.
    - Peer regulation replacing adult attunement.
4. **Model corrective adult response.** Include examples of:
    - Boundary-setting without shame.
    - Conversations about body autonomy.
    - Repair after discipline.

Why this matters:
Without this framing, clinicians in training may internalize the very biases they are meant to unlearn.

---

2. No Crease in My Shoes

Primary focus: Poverty, shame, masculinity, peer ridicule, delayed gratification, and consumer identity.

What happens:

- Amari is bullied for wearing worn-out shoes.
- His desire for status leads to poor financial decisions.

- A well-meaning adult offers guidance that is ignored.
- New shoes fail quickly, reinforcing regret.
- A caregiver reframes the experience as a lesson in patience and decision-making.

What the story is really about:

- Scarcity mindset.
- Social humiliation.
- The psychological cost of visible poverty.
- Short-term relief versus long-term consequences.
- Parent-child relational repair.

Arc 2: *No Crease in My Shoes*

Core Clinical Issues

- Scarcity mindset.
- Shame and social comparison.
- Masculinity and worth are linked to material status.
- Executive functioning under chronic stress.

Clinical Risks if Unframed

- Moralizing financial decisions.
- Overemphasis on "personal responsibility."
- Underestimation of shame-driven cognition.
- Oversimplified "lesson learned" narrative.

Clinical Recommendations

1. **Name scarcity explicitly.**
   Scarcity narrows decision-making capacity. This is well established in behavioral science and must be stated.
2. **Reframe impulsivity as stress-based cognition.**
   The child is not reckless. He is responding to a social threat.
3. **Highlight caregiver attunement over outcome.**
   The most clinically relevant moment is relational repair, not the shoe failure.
4. **Avoid tidy resolution.**
   Clinically, shame does not resolve in one incident. Emphasize ongoing vulnerability.

Why this matters:
Clinicians who miss the dynamics of scarcity risk reinforcing shame rather than building capacity.

---

3. Can You See That?

Primary focus: Undiagnosed learning disabilities, behavior as communication, and adult misinterpretation.

What happens:

- Cardy is labeled as aggressive and defiant.
- Her bullying masks literacy and vision deficits.
- A bus driver notices what the school staff missed.
- The child is evaluated, receives glasses, and behavior improves.
- Peer relationships shift once the root issue is addressed.

What the story is really about:

- Dyslexia and vision impairment.
- Mislabeling children of color.
- The school-to-punishment pipeline.
- The power of attuned adults outside formal authority roles.

Arc 3: *Can You See That?*

Core Clinical Issues

- Undiagnosed learning and sensory impairments.
- Mislabeling of behavior.
- School-to-punishment pipeline.
- Protective factors outside formal authority.

Clinical Risks if Unframed

- Overconfidence in single-factor explanations.
- Minimizing cumulative misinterpretation trauma.

- Treating assessment as a "fix" rather than a doorway.

Clinical Recommendations

1. **Emphasize behavior as communication.**
   This arc does this well, but should name it explicitly.
2. **Highlight cumulative harm.**
   The damage occurs before the glasses. Address shame, isolation, and mistrust built over time.
3. **Model multidisciplinary response.**
   Show collaboration between educators, caregivers, and clinicians.
4. **Avoid redemption-through-diagnosis framing.**
   Diagnosis explains. It does not erase harm already done.

Why this matters:
This arc is clinically strong, but readers may overgeneralize assessment as a cure rather than a starting point.

---

4. Hoosier Daddy? / A Long Weekend

Primary focus: Family instability, food insecurity, foster care risk, violence exposure, and community intervention.

What happens:

- Multiple children navigate hunger, neglect, criminal exposure, and abandonment.
- A shoplifting incident escalates toward violence.
- Police intervention threatens child removal.
- A church-based safety net intervenes.
- The story ends with fragile hope, not resolution.

What the story is really about:

- Survival behaviors.
- Moral injury in children.
- Institutional violence versus relational intervention.
- Faith-based community as a stopgap social service system.
- Cycles of trauma and resilience.

Arc 4: *Hoosier Daddy? / A Long Weekend*

Core Clinical Issues

- Complex trauma.
- Food insecurity.
- Attachment disruption.
- Exposure to violence.
- Community-based buffering.

Clinical Risks if Unframed

- Trauma voyeurism.
- Savior narratives centered on faith institutions.
- Minimizing long-term developmental impact.
- Emotional overwhelm without processing scaffolding.

Clinical Recommendations

1. **Name complex trauma clearly.**
   These are not isolated stressors. They are layered and ongoing.
2. **Clarify limits of community intervention.**
   Churches and informal helpers buffer harm but do not replace systemic care.
3. **Avoid moral resolution.**
   Survival does not equal healing.
4. **Include clinician reflection prompts.**
   Encourage readers to notice their own rescue fantasies, despair, or numbness.

Why this matters:
Without containment, readers may leave emotionally flooded or falsely reassured.

Recurring Themes Across the Entire Book

- Poverty is a chronic stressor.
- Adults are operating in survival mode.
- Children are learning emotional regulation without models.

- Schools act as both refuges and harm sites.
- Punishment substituting for care.
- Informal helpers do what systems cannot.
- Identity confusion is shaped by race, class, and visibility.

What the Book Explicitly Claims to Do

The author is transparent:

- These stories are fictional but based on lived experience.
- The goal is **awareness and discussion**, not diagnosis.
- The book is a teaching tool for educators, clinicians, and students.
- It intentionally uses unfiltered language to reflect realism.

This is not accidental. It is a deliberate stylistic and pedagogical choice.

The Attack of the Killer Weave

Chapter 1: The Night Before School

It was a regular Sunday night for Destiny, Jada, Isabella, and Maya. Surrounding their apartment complex were sirens, loud traffic, and guys outside. They were loudly talking and drinking from brown paper bag-covered bottles. It's usually lots of fighting, walking around, and music coming from cars with big shiny wheels on them. It lasts until 2 or 3 in the morning. People in this neighborhood must endure nights like this until winter snowfall.

These girls have been best friends since kindergarten and still live in the same apartment complex. They all received new iPads and internet hotspots from the school and love video chatting while they're supposed to be sleeping. That night, everyone was awake because of the gunshots, yelling, crying, and screeching tires. Somebody got shot! The girls hear their mothers on the phone trying to find out what happened. Some skinny lady, with a dirty half shirt and loose-fitting leggings, was outside the window screaming and yelling to a group of guys, "Butterball got killed! I heard they was shooting dice, and he got shot over 5 dollars!"

"I heard he was messing with that old lady, Miss Bean, and one of her old students shot him." One of the bowtie-wearing guys said as he walked by. "Incense? Bean pie, my brother?"

"Who is Miss Bean?" someone else screamed out.

"That's the lady that be getting everybody in school and college. You know, the dark-skinned old lady that live on that corner," said a random boy on the bike. He was holding the leash of a brindle pit bull, covered in scars and cuts.

So, the girls were awake, Facetiming, giggling, and trying to find out what happened outside. They were talking about other fourth graders in their class, what they would wear the next day, and a new TikTok.

"These fools out here shooting again! I wish I could get some sleep sometimes. Maybe we can move one day." Isabella said while walking away from the window.

"Izzy! Get yo ass off that phone and brush your teeth and get in that bed!" her mom yelled while standing over the stove in the kitchen.

"OMG-uh, I hate brushing my teeth at night. I want to eat my Taki's and watch TikTok until I go to sleep." Whispered Isabella while turning up her nose and scrunching her face. Then she hurried up and started brushing her teeth.

Jada laughed and said, "Me too, girl, but it's better

than Big Back Amari loud talking about you on the bus. With his stankin' ass breath on the way to school. You know he likes you, girl."

Isabella replied, "I know, girl. He always talking about how he likes my hair. He be trying to touch it and smell it! That boy is crazy! He gets on my nerves."

Destiny, that's the one they always call bougie because they say she talks like white people. She always has her hair done and wears nice, clean, newer clothes. She also has the best reading and math scores in school. Destiny was lying in bed, smiling and saying, "I already have my pajamas on, and I'm in my bed. I will not be hearing my mother's voice this evening."

But Maya had something special planned that night. "Y'all, I'm going to be up all night. I'm getting my hair done! My momma had to leave and get another bundle so she could finish it. She's been gone a long time, though. She probably can't park nowhere because all them police is out there." Maya grandly announced while flipping her long, halfway-done, shiny new hair in front of the screen. "Wait until tomorrow. Y'all gone see."

"What's a bundle?" asked Isabella with a curious and perplexed look on her face.

Maya grinned and smirked. "Girl, you don't know? It's like a bag full of hair. My mom braids it in with my real hair. It makes it look like the hair on those girls that be twerking in the rap videos. It's the best you've ever seen! No Cap! I been in this chair all day, and my butt hurts, but when it's done, I'm gonna look like a baddie! Y'all Mexicans ain't gotta worry about that because y'all got good long hair already." Maya went on and on, bragging and boasting, then described in detail the process of getting the weave put in.

"I ain't no Mexican, I'm from Guatemala. You gone quit playing with me." Isabella said, staring into the camera with a mean look.

"Whatever, girl. Same thing…" Maya said jokingly. All the girls chuckled and continued the conversation.

Maya continued to talk about how it would make her look like all her favorite TikTok's, Instagram models, and YouTube influencers, and how she couldn't wait for her crush to look at her. The other girls were somewhat confused and a little unsure. "Girl, you doing too much. You know we got gym tomorrow. " Said Jada.

While popping her gum, twirling her curly locs, and looking in the camera with duck lips, Isabella said,

“For real though, I'm just glad I got my regular hair. We ain’t gotta do all that."

Maya’s mom, Angel, finally makes it home with the bundles, but her eyes are red, and she looks exhausted. She smells like the same smoke as the men outside. Maya knows not to question her mom because there is a strong possibility she could get smacked in the mouth. So, she quietly comes out of her room and, with a fearful tone, says, “Hey, Momma. You, ok? Are you gonna finish my hair?”

“I’m good. I had to make a run real quick, though. Let me finish your hair so we can both go to bed. I didn’t get everything I needed, but it’s still gonna look good. Just put your head on my lap like this and be still. I’ll be done before you know it.” Angel said while sitting down on the couch with a pillow in her lap.

Relieved and closing her eyes, Maya said, “Ok, thanks, Momma. I love you.”

Chapter 2: Dreamland

That night, while Destiny, Jada, and Isabella dreamed about wearing new clothes, eating their favorite food, having fun at the park, and flying through the air at Sky Zone, but Maya had a different dream. While lying on her mom’s lap, she fell asleep getting her hair done. She envisioned herself going viral for her

TikTok dance, with her hair whipping back and forth! Cameras flashed, and a large crowd screamed as she wore a glittery half-shirt, tight red shorts, and high-heeled boots to match the color of her hair. She could see her face was a billboard on the side of the JW Marriott downtown. She was performing inside Lucas Oil Stadium, flipping her hair, dancing, and singing while holding a golden, glittery microphone. Maya could see herself on the Jumbotron. Everyone was awestruck by her dance moves and the way her weave blew in the wind, reminiscent of Beyoncé. She made it! Everybody knew her and was screaming her name. MAYA…MAYA…MAYA…MAYA! Now she was more famous than Taylor Swift!

But in the middle of her dream, something strange happened. She was getting so hot and feeling intense heat from all the lights and camera flashes. As she was taking pics with the fans, her head started to itch. She scratched and scratched, then patted her head repeatedly, but it wouldn't stop! Suddenly, glue started dripping down her face like candle wax, and the weave in her dream started to come out. The crowd began to "BOOOOO" at her loudly and violently until she was bald! Maya woke up sweating and crying. She reached under her bonnet to check on her weave. "Woooooo! Thank God it's still on!"

She glanced at the clock on her mother's phone,

which read 6:12 am. Maya thought to herself, "It's time to get up at 6:30. I might as well get up now, while everybody still sleep." Maya rose from her sleeping mother's lap with a line of slobber connected to the pillow, got off the couch, and quietly went to the refrigerator. "Dang-uh…it ain't never nothing to eat in here," Maya whispered, in fear of waking up her mother. Then she thought to herself, "Oh well. I'll eat at school. But first, I need to put on that shirt Momma wears that shows her belly ring. I know it's here somewhere." Maya quietly tiptoes into her mother's bedroom and rummages through her mom's drawer, with no luck. "Dang-uh!"

Chapter 3: Morning Mayhem

That morning, Destiny, Jada, and Isabella woke up and started their morning routine as usual. — brushing teeth, washing faces, putting on their clothes, fixing their hair, grabbing their backpacks, and getting ready for the school bus. But Maya's morning was a little more complex than usual. As she got up and started getting ready, she kept complaining to her mom. "Momma, it itches so much!"

Angel shook her head in disgust, speaking loudly and impatiently. "You're the one who asked for this hair! You don't know what I had to do to get that money! I paid 100 dollars for that hair, so stop complaining."

Angel looks at Maya as her eyes begin to water and says, "Sorry for yelling, but I've got to go to work. Girl, you'll get used to it soon. You can't scratch it though, or you'll mess up your weave. Just pat it."

"Pat it? How? Like this?" Maya, looking into her mother's eyes, confused, tried what she thought was right. She repeatedly smacks herself on the head over and over and over in the same spot, but now her head hurts even more. With tears in her eyes, "This is the worst!" she grumbled under her breath. Maya angrily walked away toward the bathroom to finish getting ready for school. When Maya glanced in the mirror, she instantly remembered why she was going through all this pain. "Damn, I look good af!" She said to the reflection in the mirror. "Aww yeah, these hoes gone be hating. I'm an official baddie!"

While in the bathroom, Maya finishes getting dressed and is singing her favorite Sexyy Red song:

"Slim thick, caramel skin, 5'5" this Bitch a 10

Hair done, bills paid, catch me slidin' in a Benz (Vyoom)

I ain't lookin' for no man... Ain't recruitin' no new friends

Louis bag filled with bands

Go on, Sexyy, do your dance

Uh, uh (Get it, Sexyy), uh, uh (Get it Sexyy)."

As Angel walks by the door, she hears Maya and yells, “HEY!!! WHAT YOU IN THERE SAYING? LISTEN HERE LITTLE GIRL, YOU BETTER NOT LET ME CATCH YOU REPEATING THAT NASTY GIRL’S RAP SONG AGAIN. NOW GET YOUR BUTT TO THAT BUS STOP! NOW!”

Startled and afraid, Maya jumped, then said, “Sorry, momma. I’m hurrying up.”

Upon arrival at the bus stop, Maya wasn't as friendly as usual. Instead, she acted like a reality show star of "Bad Girls Club", her face scrunched up, flipping her hair and bragging about how she looked like Sexyy Redd. But the other girls were already tired of her stank attitude.

"Uh, Maya, you doing too much!" stated Jada while rolling her eyes.

"You just hating," Maya snapped her fingers and flipped her hair again. "I'm just too turned up."

Chapter 4: Trouble at School

Maya pushed her way in front of her friends to get on the bus first. “I’m the baddest bitch, so I get to go first!” she said. All the other students waiting for the bus couldn’t believe she was acting this way toward them. No one spoke up until...

"You ain't nothing! Just because you got fake hair... That's why I saw your momma with my uncle and them last night. You know what they be doin'!" said Ty with the side eye.

With her hand in his face and rolling her eyes, Maya replied. "Shut up and mind your business, little boy." She climbed the stairs and continued walking down the aisle of the school bus like it was a runway during fashion week in Paris. Maya was twisting her hips and winking at the other boys on the bus until she got to her seat. When she sat down, Maya ignored everyone, pulled out her phone, and started looking at herself, making what she thought were sexy faces, then went back to singing her favorite song with her hands up and snapping her fingers. *"Get it, Sexyy! Get it Sexyy!... Aye... Aye…"*

Once they got to school, some kids and teachers noticed Maya's new hairstyle. Some said it looked nice, but others didn't care. Maya, walking with her head held high and a scrunched-up, mean girl face, soaking up all the compliments and barely saying thank you to anyone. She even started to ignore her friends.

After the announcements and Pledge of Allegiance, Maya began to worry about gym class. She doesn't want to sweat and mess up her hair. Then she thought back to the conversation she had with the girls last night and thought, “Oh no! We gotta swim today! Dang-uh!! I just ain’t going. F it!”

“Okay, class, line up for gym!” Ms. White said. “I want all of you to have fun today and be really careful. Partner up and let’s head to the pool.” All the students were searching for eye contact with anyone who wanted to be their partner. Some students paired up quickly, while others had to wait and find a partner from the remaining students who were standing with their heads down.

Korbyn nervously said in a hushed tone, “Hey Maya. Your hair looks pretty. Will you be my partner today?”

Maya, attempting to embarrass Korbyn, yelled out, “Hell naw, little boy. I ain’t being your damn partner. I don’t even need a partner today!”

Korbyn, feeling full of shame and embarrassment, put his head down and walked to the back of the line until he heard, “Bro, just come over here with me. I got you.” Amari showed empathy when he saw Korbyn feeling bad and wanted to help him.

In gym class, things got worse. Maya had a serious choice to make. Her mom told her she better not mess up that weave. "I can't swim today," Maya said dramatically, as she paced back and forth with folded arms. "I can't get my hair wet." But the other kids were so excited. They all ran and jumped into the pool, splashing each other, screaming and laughing. Maya stood on the side, face still scrunched up, looking miserable.

Eventually, she couldn't resist the fun, and gym time was running out. "I don't care no more, I'm swimming!" she shouted as she jumped into the pool. Her face was filled with joy again. Maya was smiling and talking to the other students. But as soon as she went underwater, the weave started to come out. First, it just looked crooked on her head, then it began to turn into a big curly ball. "Woooooo!! This fun!" Maya yelled out, then went underwater one more time and came up without her weave. She had no idea what was going on. She just started being nice and participating with the other students.

No one noticed, but the weave had a mind of its own. It sank deep like a heavy bag of sand, toward the bottom of the pool. Then suddenly, it took off like a torpedo through the water, weaving through the kids, looking for someone to latch onto. The kids were playing and splashing so much that they didn't even notice it. Her weave finally swam into the deep end like a jellyfish. And when swimming class was over, it waited at the bottom of the pool.

Maya got out of the pool, and a few kids started to snicker and laugh. "What's funny?" Maya asked.

Korbyn pointed and replied, "Your hair is gone! You can't feel it?"

Maya touched her head to check if it was true. She rubbed and rubbed, but the hair was gone. "Oh well. I had fun." Maya said. She felt embarrassed but also a little relieved. "I'm cool on that weave. It wasn't worth all this. I'll take my punishment," she thought to herself.

Chapter 5: The Weave Strikes Again

After discovering her weave was missing, Korbyn and Maya tried to retrieve it so she could return it to her mother and explain what happened. But the weave had swam to the bottom of the deep end, and they couldn't get it. Every time they tried to use the pool skimmer net to get it, the weave would move. "Forget it. We gotta get dressed and get back to class. We can't be late, or we can't have recess today." Korbyn said.

The weave wasn't finished! It wants to stay alive, and it's ready to cause more trouble. The weave has a life of its own! It has some magical powers and somehow remained in the pool, waiting for its next victim.

Meanwhile, another class is preparing for gym time. While walking down the hallway, Amari spots his crush, Isabella. All the boys start teasing Amari because they know he has feelings for her. Amari breaks away from the group into a light jog and says, "Hi, Isabella. You look so pretty. I love your hair. Let me touch it!" Amari has the biggest grin, showing all his teeth. As he attempted to walk with her down the hallway, he said, "Where is your class going for specials?"

"Amari. Please don't distract me. I'm thinking about my test later today. But if you must know, I'm going to gym class." Said Isabella, blushing and slightly embarrassed.

"Okay, cool. I'll see you in the pool. Hey, that rhymed!" Amari held his stomach and laughed. "Can I play the splash games with you when we get free time?" He anxiously asked.

With a devilish grin and educated tone, Isabella flipped her hair and stated, "You're so immature for your age… Maybe. Now, please allow me to proceed to class without interruption!"

Ironically, Isabella has swimming in gym for the next class. When Isabella jumped into the pool, she was having the time of her life! She loves water and is very nice to all her friends. They played splash games, which made her incredibly happy. Before the class ended, Isabella wanted to show the others she could dive in the deep end. Isabella ran off the diving board, jumped, and made a perfect dive.

The evil weave spotted its next victim, Isabella! It swam to her faster than a shark and attacked! The weave latched onto her hair while she was underwater. When she climbed out of the pool, the weave was stuck to her head!

At first, because she has long hair, no one noticed, not even Isabella. But before she dried off, her attitude changed, just like Maya's had. She began to act rudely, ignoring her friends and twisting her hips as she walked. With a shocked and disappointed look, Amari said, "Isabella? What's wrong with you? Why you acting like that?"

Isabella yelled out, "Boy, leave me the F alone!"

The entire class was awestruck! They couldn't believe it. Isabella was cursing. She even attempted to perform inappropriate dance moves in front of everyone, which landed her in trouble with the teacher. Isabella was bending over with her legs open, touching her toes and saying,
"Aye…Aye…Aye…Aye. Look y'all! I'm twerkin'! I'm dancing like a stripper!" While shaking her head 'no', the swimming instructor, Ms. Kirsten, said, "Isabella! Why are you acting like that? You know better."

"Like what?" Isabella snapped back, with her hand on her hips and rolling her eyes. "You need to mind your business, old bitch!"

The entire class gasped collectively, "Huuuuuuuuuuuh…"

"You are always the sweetest and nicest to everyone. You're the best student in the school. I'm disappointed in you. Go dry off and get dressed. I'm sending you to the office!" Ms. Kirsten said.

All the students were in shock. They couldn't believe what they were seeing. Amari walked away in disbelief, with his head down and grumbling to himself, "I don't like her no more. She's acting crazy. I ain't liking no girls with weave. They be doing too much."

Chapter 6: Unknown Consequences

The principal, Ms. Preston, called Isabella's mother to come to the school for her behavior. Her mother could not believe Isabella was acting out.

"Hello. Can I speak to Ms. Ana Perez? This is Principal Preston from school 105." There was a whispering voice on the other end of the call.

"Hi. Just hold on one second." No cell phones are allowed while Ms. Perez is at work. So, she says to the other workers, "Hey, can y'all cover me real quick? I need to go to the bathroom." Once she gets inside, she replies to Ms. Preston. "Sorry about that, I'm at work, and we're not supposed to be on the phone. Is everything okay?"

Ms. Preston went on to say, "Okay, I'll make it quick. Isabella cursed at her teacher today and misbehaved in swimming class. Now, because she never gets in trouble, I'll need you to come pick her up from school. I won't put it in her records that she has a suspension, but you still need to come get her."

"Not my Isabella! She is the top student in this school and never gets into trouble. I'm leaving work right now!" Mom hung up and anxiously went to tell her manager what happened.

"Sean, I need to leave to get my daughter from school. She's in trouble," said Ana.

With skepticism, her manager, Sean, stated, "What? Now? It's the lunch rush! We need everybody right now. I can't let you leave. There is no one to cover your shift. If you leave, you will have to find another job. I need dependable people. So, what are you going to do?"

Mom started to cry, but she had to make a decision. She decided to plead for her job. "Please just give me one more chance. I never come in late or miss work. Just this one time, please!?"

Sean stood on business and said, "No! You know the rules. If you leave, you're fired. I'm sorry."

Mom left her job devastated, but knew the bus was only one minute away. She gathered her things as quickly as she could, bolted out the door, ran to the corner, and got on the city bus just in time. Once she caught her breath and realized she wouldn't be able to pay her bills, she broke down in tears all the way to the school.

The bus lets her off about a block from the school. That gave her enough time to dry her tears and wipe off her face before entering the school. She became angry and started talking to herself. "I can't believe this little girl is here acting a fool. I done lost my job, and I'm beating her butt when we get home." Mom sadly walked into the school and asked for Ms. Preston. The receptionist, Miss Carla, showed her to the principal's office. When she opened the door, she gasped and yelled at the sight of the weave. "What is that thing in your head?!"

Isabella looked perplexed and stated, "What is you talking about? Anyway, did you bring me some tacos? I'm hungry!"

Mom frantically walked over to Isabella, snatched that "thing" off her head, and threw it on the ground. "No Taco Bell for you! I got fired today because I had to come to the school to address your behavior. I'm so disappointed in you."

Isabella was foggy and confused. She didn't know what was going on. Ms. Perez grabbed her by the arm, pulled her out of her seat, and headed toward the door. "Momma! Momma! What I do?" Isabella pleaded as if she were crying for mercy.

"I'm getting ready to beat that butt when we get home. You just wait!" Mom whispered to her.

Ms. Preston turned around to close her door and pick up the weave from the ground, but it was gone! She doesn't know what happened to it. Ms. Preston, talking to herself, said, "That's crazy! I thought that weave was just right here. Well, maybe her mom took it. Anyway, it's gone."

The weave is on the loose and looking for another victim!

Chapter 7: A Lesson Learned

It was finally time for lunch, and all four girls usually sit together in the cafeteria. They are very hungry because they attend the last lunch period of the day. Today, only three of the girls were at the table, but they were relieved that the weave was finally gone. Destiny and Jada noticed how calm Maya was.

While looking at herself and fixing her hair in the reflection of the window they were sitting by, Destiny said, "We heard you all were antagonizing people and really going overboard with the antics today. They said Isabella was cursing and dancing inappropriately in the gym. I think people call it ‘twerking’. And Maya, you were just out of control the entire day."

"I ain't never getting weave again," Maya said, laughing. “I had to pat my head to stop it from itching most of the time anyway. My teacher said to stop before I get a concussion.”

"Yeah, I bet Isabella ain’t either. We have no idea how that thing ended up on her head. But I heard her momma dragged her and pulled out a belt and whooped her in the office today!" Jada said. Then all the girls laughed. “I wonder why we always eat lunch, and then it's time to go home. I be hungry all day. Let’s get those extras out of the bucket and take them home. They be bussin’ when I get home and be hungry.”

“That idea ate!” said Destiny. “Let’s do it!”

Only an hour and a half after lunch, the final bell rang, and the school day was over. Miss Carla makes the end-of-the-day announcements over the loudspeaker, and at the end she says, "Purple bus riders, line up!" As the girls were lined up and moving to the hallway, they spotted Cardy in the other bus line wearing the weave. She was mean, cursing, and had a bad attitude. She was strutting around and whipping her hair back and forth like an IG model.

Maya said with a perplexed facial expression, "Look, y'all. She got on my weave from earlier. I wonder how she got it?" All the girls looked at each other, shook their heads, and shrugged their shoulders.

Jada stated, "Who knows and who cares. That's so cringe. She gonna find out, though. I ain't never getting no weave!" All the girls smiled, glad to have learned their lesson. "We're sticking with our natural hair from now on, deal?" In unison, the others nodded in agreement and said, "True!"

Did you know: *"A host of dangerous chemicals, including carcinogens, lead, and volatile organic compounds (VOCs), have been found in some of the most popular synthetic hair brands used in braided styles.*

The findings were detailed in a Feb. 27, 2025, article in Consumer Reports.

Synthetic braiding hair is widely used by Black people, mostly women. Some people experience skin issues such as redness, swelling, and rashes while wearing braids. And while there is a lack of research on the long-term risks posed by synthetic braids, the chemicals they contain have been linked with a number of serious health harms.

Consumer Reports tested ten synthetic braiding hair

products—and found toxins in all ten. For example, three products contained benzene, a carcinogen which has been linked with acute myeloid leukemia. Nine out of ten products contained unsafe levels of lead, which in adults can cause kidney damage, cardiovascular problems, reproductive damage, and brain damage, and in children can lead to brain and nervous system damage, learning disabilities, behavioral problems, and developmental delays. The VOC found at the highest levels in the hair products was acetone, a respiratory irritant."

Harvard T. H. Chan School of Public Health, March 5, 2025

General Discussion:

1. What did you notice about their environment? How does this affect people's behavior?
2. Which character(s) could you coach to a better outcome? What practical steps would you advise?
3. Does a lack of literacy and communication skills affect any situation? How? Why?
4. Children often mimic adult behavior. Identify and discuss the positive and the negative behaviors you noticed.
5. What would be considered a proper age for a child to wear synthetic hair on their head? Why?

Clinical Discussion by Dr. Calvin Spinks:

Part 1: Story Engagement

- What about their story reminded you of yourself or someone you know?
- Which character's choices made you feel proud, confused, or frustrated?

2. What was the central conflict? How did each girl respond to it?

- Was the conflict about the weave, or something deeper?
- Who changed the most, and what helped them shift?

3. What nonverbal cues helped you understand what the characters were feeling?

- Think about tone, body language, and silence.
- When Maya said "Dang-uh" in the fridge or when she rubbed her scalp, what was going on under the surface?

Part 2: Cultural and Clinical Processing

4. How do beauty standards show up in the story?

- What messages were the girls receiving about their natural hair?

- What were they hoping to gain by changing their look?

5. What roles did adults play in either reinforcing or challenging those messages?

- Did any adult notice what the girls were *really* going through?
- Who tried to help? Who missed the signs?

6. If you were working with Maya or Isabella as a counselor, mentor, or teacher, what would you do differently?

- What questions would you ask to build trust?
- What behaviors might be trauma responses instead of misbehavior?

7. How can we talk to kids about beauty, identity, and health in ways that affirm them instead of shaming them?

- What might you say to a child who feels that "looking good" is the only way to be respected or seen?

Part 3: Public Health and Structural Thinking

8. What do you make of the fact that every tested braid hair sample contained toxins?

- Why do you think these products are so widely used, even if they might be unsafe?

9. How does this relate to broader issues of environmental racism and neglect?

- Think about food deserts, hair product safety, or housing conditions. Who gets left behind, and why?

Optional Wrap-Up Activities

A. Role Play: Trauma-Informed Conversation
Pick one character (Maya, Isabella, or Korbyn). Imagine you're their school counselor. How would you respond to what happened? What would you say first?

B. Creative Reflection
Write a short letter from the weave itself, explaining why it acts the way it does. What would the weave say about the pressure these kids are under?

C. Action Step
What's one thing schools, clinics, or parents could do to support healthier conversations about hair, identity, and belonging?

Questions posed by Dr. Sonya Berle, DSW, LICSW, CADAC IV, ASID Associate.

Cultural and Clinical Processing

1. When pondering stereotyping and the "isms," can you provide an example of seemingly automatic thoughts verbalized/communicated from one story character to another?

2. If we look at the weave's magic symbolically and apply a mental health lens to the magic, what symptoms can you notice a weave wearer experiencing? For example, do you see a sudden onset of mood changes? Next, think about and discuss the effects of symptomology on the youth experiencing it in real time and on the people in their environment (peers, teachers, family members). What diagnosis might you explore, and what might you rule out based on presenting symptoms?

Public Health and Structural Thinking

1. Can you examine Maya's food scarcity presented in Chapter Two? What barrier experiences and resiliency-based thinking do you notice in Maya? What resources are available that help Maya shift from concerns about hunger to the next steps of getting ready for school? Secondly, please ponder the importance of continued federal and state funding for food programs and consider how Maya's

resiliency-based thinking might look different if those programs were cut.

2. Please refer to the Reflections Key (SDOH, Learning Section p.162) and think from a neuroscience lens. The students in this story do not eat lunch until 90 minutes before school dismisses. If basic needs are not met while a student is attempting to assimilate new learning (at school), what happens to the quality of those cognitive tasks? What brain centers are necessary for cognition? Are they the same brain centers and ratios of use needed for survival mode to meet basic needs? Are the parts of the brain and functions complementary? Contradictory? Or both?

3. Consider Isabella's mother; what action-oriented and verbalized core values are thwarted by systemic and environmental stressors? Consider the layers of her job loss on self-image, values, and identity, too.

No Crease in My Shoes

"Oppressed youth often develop what I call a cultural camouflage. It's not who they are. It's who they think they have to be in order to get through the day." Dr. Kenneth Hardy

Chapter 1: The Long Ride Home

It was so loud in the hallway. Kids were screaming and yelling, playfully pushing and shoving, just to get in line for the dismissal. The teachers were visibly exhausted and losing their voices from all the yelling. The announcements started notifying buses' dismissals by color. "Teachers, please send all the purple bus riders to the front!" Ms. Carla said over the intercom.

As the students walked in single file toward the stairs, all they could hear was Cardy. She was popping her gum, laughing loudly at everything, bullying the younger kids to move out of her way, and swinging her book bag around like a force field.

"Look at his shoes!" Cardy yelled out as she pointed downward toward Amari's shoes. He had on old gym shoes with a hole in the bottom of one, showing his sock, creases on the top so deep near the toe that it looked like a curled-up witch's boot, and mismatched brown shoelaces that may have been white a long time ago. One shoestring was shorter than the other, so he couldn't tie it. Amari busted the seams on the other shoe, so when he walked, they would come apart. Everyone in line looked down at Amari's shoes and started pointing and laughing uncontrollably.

The teacher, Ms. White, told Cardy to be quiet and show respect to other students. Cardy, with one hand on her hip, whipping her head, rolled her eyes and said, "Whatever…You get on my nerves." Ms. White pulled her out of line, escorted her to the bus, and told the bus driver, "She's been acting up. Please make her sit in the back so she doesn't bother the other students."

Amari was somewhat relieved but still embarrassed. He felt bad but still said goodbye to his friends and teachers. With his head up, holding back his tears as if he was going to cry, he said, "See y'all tomorrow." Amari chatted with his friends on his way to the bus, unaware that the mean girl, Cardy, was waiting for him. When getting on the bus, all anyone could see was her big hair and evil eyes peaking over the last seat on the school bus.

Amari strategically strolled and chatted with his peers, just so the others could get on the bus, and he wouldn't have to sit in the back beside Cardy. He finally boarded the bus, only to realize his plan had backfired! There was only one seat left. The seat was right in front of Cardy! He walked even more slowly, like he was walking the plank in an old pirate movie. Today, the sound of the school bus door closing was like a prison cell shutting behind him. *CLANK!* Amari had only taken two steps past the bus driver, then *GULP!* He took a heavy swallow and heard…

"Look at Amari's shoes, y'all! They flappin' like they talking to somebody!" a loud voice rang out.

GULP! Amari took another hard swallow and deep breath, then tried to ignore her. But he was frozen like a statue, squeezing his backpack and hiding his shoes by walking as fast as he could to the last available seat on the bus. That voice was so familiar. He knew precisely who it was-Cardy, the queen mean girl! Once he finally got seated, he put his head down and sighed. Amari tried looking out of the window and thinking about something else, but it didn't work. Cardy was making the entire bus laugh all the way home.

"What's up with those shoes, my boy? They got big creases in them. We just gonna call them slip and slides because you be slipping and sliding when you play in the gym!" she jokingly cackled. "They look like you just got those out of the trash!"

The bus erupted in screams and laughter. Amari, with his eyes watering again, ground his teeth, grew increasingly angry and frustrated. He remembered his coping skills and took a few deep breaths, unballed his fists, and kept quiet. Amari was thinking of all the bad things he wanted to happen to Cardy. He thought to himself, “I hate this girl! I hope the emergency door opens and she falls out!” Amari chuckled to himself, finding a bit of relief from his anxiety.

“What you laughin’ at, fool? You had them shoes since the first day of school!” Cardy continued to tease and laugh.

“I bet I got on new shoes tomorrow, watch,” Amari whispered back, but no one could really hear him. The laughter and pointing quieted down, and for a moment, Amari was relieved it was over—until Cardy shouted.

“I got on the new J’s! They cost $200. What you gonna get? Y’all broke!” The crowd responded with a long, loud “Ooooooooooooooo” as most of the students got off the bus at their apartment complex.

Ty and Amari’s stop was next. As soon as the bus

stopped, Amari felt the pain in his chest start to go away. He had to walk from the back of the bus, ashamed of his shoes. Amari had his head down, trying to ignore the whispers and laughs. To make matters worse, once he got off the bus, he tripped on the last step and fell into a puddle. All the remaining kids on the bus laughed and pointed as the bus drove away.

"Get up, man. You alright. Don't worry about them, bro." Ty said. "I got an extra coat and some jeans my brother left when he got locked up. You can have those if you want. I ain't got no extra shoes though."

Amari's feet and socks were wet from the big hole in the bottom of his shoe. His pants and coat were soggy and muddy. Amari just looked up in the air for God to save him and began to cry. "I hate this. When I get older, I ain't never gonna have old shoes!"

Ty agreed. As they walked away toward the trash-filled parking lot, on the way to their apartments, he said, "Me either, bro! I'm gonna be in the NFL, a policeman, or a YouTuber. I'm going to be rich." The boys finished their walk to Ty's house, daydreaming together in silence. As Amari stopped sniffling and wiped his face, Ty said, "I'll be right back with those clothes. My mom said I can't have nobody in here until she comes home, so chill right here."

Meanwhile, Amari waited by the front door, anticipating the arrival of new clothes and a coat. He had a quick daydream that he was getting new pants, Jordans, a matching hat, and a long shiny chain like the rappers on TikTok. Amari could hear the music inside Ty's house, and he smelled the weird smoke he sometimes smelled at home. After a few minutes of dreaming about how cool he would look in his new clothes, Ty came out and said, "Here you go, my boy! This is all I could find, but if I get some more, I got you!"

Amari excitedly grabbed the clothes and said, "Thanks, bro!" Then he walked to the next building to his apartment. "Finally!" Amari said as he dropped his bag of clothes and backpack by the door. He was thrilled to be home, but his hunger soon caught up with him. He went to the kitchen and started to boil water for Top Ramen noodles. "Dang! Ain't nothing to eat but the red packs. Mom probably ate the orange and pink ones. I guess I'll eat these and put some hot sauce on them." They were beef-flavored, but he didn't care today.

After 5 minutes of stirring the noodles in the hot

water, they were ready to go. Amari used a fork to check if the noodles were soft and ready to eat. He got a small forkful and put it in his mouth. "Ah shit…these too hot!" Amari said. He had his mouth open, trying to fan the inside with his hand, hoping he could chew it down easier. He poured the rest of the noodles into a bowl, frantically trying to dump hot sauce on them, but there wasn't enough in the bottle.

One time, he saw his momma take the cap off a ketchup bottle, run a little water from the faucet into it, shake it up, and then pour it on her food. He tried this method with the hot sauce. "I think this how you make more hot sauce." He said to himself, then he poured the watered-down hot sauce on his noodles. "Yummm. I'm ready to smash. This is bussin'." He sat down on the bean bag to eat. As he let the noodles cool off, he started playing on his phone and watching TikTok. Amari knew his mom was coming home soon.

Chapter 2: The Mall Trip

When his mom, Sharman, finally walked through the door, she was exhausted. She took off her wig and shoes, and before she sat on the couch, walked to the kitchen and began making a drink from a brown bottle she kept above the refrigerator. "Woo Lord! I'm tired, son. The other lady didn't come to work, so I had to clean the whole building by myself. How you doing today, son?" she said, while pulling a small, brown, half-smoked cigar and a lighter from her shirt pocket. "You do your schoolwork today?"

Amari was nervous and hesitant. "It was... okay. But when we going to the mall? You said I could get new shoes. Look!" Amari shows his mom that the sole of his shoe is coming off, and there is a hole in the bottom of the other one. "I need them bad! Momma, please!"

Sharman took a deep breath, sighed, and rubbed her eyes. "Amari, I'm tired. I been on my feet for 12 hours. Can you wait until tomorrow? Better yet, Friday is probably best. I get paid that day."

"Please, Momma," Amari begged, his eyes watering and voice trembling. "I can't wear these no more. My feet keep getting wet, and I'm always sliding and falling in the gym when I play basketball. Please, ma! I won't ask for nothing else."

Sharman glanced at him for a quick second, feeling tired and defeated. She said, "Gimme a minute to finish my drink and use the bathroom, then I'll be ready."

Amari was so happy! He had the biggest smile, as if he had just won a Grammy award! He went to grab his new coat from the trash bag of clothes and got ready to go. He knew she would be in there for a while. Amari can smell that weird aroma coming from the bathroom. Amari said to himself, "I hate that kind of smoke. It stays in the bathroom for a long time." The smoke made him cough, so he grabbed his old basketball and dribbled it outside. Amari was perfecting his signature moves, dreaming of one day playing in the NBA and securing his own shoe contract. Sharman came out 15 minutes later, walking slowly, but very calm, and said, "I'm ready now. Let's hurry and get to this bus stop before we miss it."

The bus ride to the mall seemed like an eternity. It took three transfers! Amari leaned against his mom, talking nonstop about the type of shoes he wanted. "I might get some LaMelo Balls, or some Kobe's. Maybe the Currys. Oh, I know, the Jordan 11's—they're the best!"

Sharman, sitting there in a daze, smiled but didn't say much. When they finally reached the mall, Amari's excitement bubbled over. As soon as those bus doors opened, Amari jumped like a grasshopper off the bus to the sidewalk. He ran ahead and said, "Come on,

Mom. Hurry up! I want to show you the LaMelo Ball shoes!" Amari ran to the store as fast as he could, looking back to see if his mom was keeping up.

"Slow down, boy! I'm coming." Sharman said with a laughing smile on her face. "Boy, you fast like your uncle Reggie!"

Chapter 3: Make good decisions

"Hey! Welcome to Baller Shoes. My name is Blake. What are you looking for today?" said the sales manager. Amari was speechless and in awe, looking at all the gym shoes on the wall.

Amari turned to the right and saw lights coming from the ceiling. The light was shining down on a glass case with a gleaming white pair of J's inside. These are the shoes he'd seen on TikTok ads and on his classmates' feet. He turned to his mom, beaming with joy and flashing his cheesy smile. Amari looked at his mom with the look of desperation of a starving child and said, "Look! These the ones I want, Mom! These go hard!"

She glanced at the price tag and shook her head. "$193.99? Baby, I don't get paid until Friday. I only have $100 for the week. We can only spend about $60 today."

Amari's heart sank into his chest, and his attitude changed. That big, beautiful smile quickly turned upside down. He started folding his arms, and he poked out his bottom lip. He was so disappointed. Knowing that kids at school might laugh at his shoes, he started to lobby for the best shoes he could get. "I can't get nothing for $60. I can't wear no more cheap shoes! I can't run fast or jump high in them. Momma, please!?"

Sharman knelt and looked him in the eye and explained, "I know it's hard, but we have to be smart. If you wait until Friday, they might be on sale. You could get these or even something better."

Blake was listening to the conversation and said, "Hey, lil man. Those will be on sale on Friday but let me go to the back and see what we got. You look like a size 6. Let me check your size. Take your shoe off."

Amari looked more frightened than ever. He knew he had mismatched holey socks that he hadn't changed in three days. Amari is facing a huge dilemma. He can't remember which sock has the most enormous hole! He takes off his left shoe, then he thinks, "Oh, no! I hate this!" His big toe, with a dirty toenail, poked out of his sock like a turtle's head protruding from its shell. Amari looked down, and a tear rolled down his right cheek.

Blake looked down, winked at him, smiled, then said, "Don't worry, lil man, I throw in some socks for you. It's on me. Looks like you're a size 8 though."

Amari began to wish, hope, and pray that he would return with something good. He started walking around the store, watching as other kids got what they wanted, which only made him angrier. Amari whispered to himself, "Please God, let him bring back something good. I don't never get nothing I want."

Blake emerged from the back, peeking over the top of 5 multicolored boxes stacked like cinder blocks. With a very positive attitude and tone of voice, he said, "Yo lil man! I got a few nice pairs. Check these out." Amari walked over with his head down and a sad face, still hoping he could get something good. Blake says, "These Iversons are nice. Someone brought them back because they didn't fit. Try them on."

Sharman says, "Those are nice! I like those. You should get them. They only $55.99. That's in our budget."

Amari's face scrunched up, and with a bad attitude,

stated, "Who is Iverson? He ain't nobody. I ain't never heard of them shoes. You got something else?"

Blake giggled and excitedly said, "You never heard of Allen Iverson? He was one of the best to ever play in the NBA! He was an MVP! He was small and fast, just like you! These shoes were $179.99, and now they're marked down. It's a really good deal." Mom and Blake tried to convince Amari, but he would not budge. He stood there, arms crossed, shaking his head 'no' and refused to try them on or even look at them again. Mom said, "Don't forget, you could wait until Friday and get the J's. They'll be on sale then."

Blake opened up all the other boxes. After a quick scan of all the shoes, Amari's eyes lit up! "What about those? They look just like the J's, but the man on the side of the shoe is a little different. What are those called?" Amari asked with a very curious look on his face. Blake laughed a little bit and said, "Nah, lil bro, you don't want them. They're called Jumps. They look aight, but those aren't the best quality. Get the Iversons! They're the same price!"

Amari thought about the kids on the bus and Cardy's voice echoing in his head. He didn't want to wait anymore. "I'm getting those Jumps. They look just like the J's. No one will even know."

Amari was excited and happy. He started telling his mom stories about how all the kids would love his shoes and how great he'd look on the basketball court tomorrow. His mom, Sharman, patted his shoulder and said, "You can't worry about what other people think of you. People will tease you no matter what you wear or do. Some people are just petty like that." He nodded yes, convinced that these new shoes would finally get Cardy to leave him alone when he got on the school bus tomorrow.

Chapter 4: It's Showtime!

That night before bed, he had the "Jumps" out and sitting on top of the shoe box, laced up and ready to go. He put them on multiple times, trying different ways to lace them up. He wanted to see what they looked like on his feet, but the bathroom mirror was too high. Amari used his mom's phone to take some pics to get a better view. "Hell yeah!" he whispered to himself while looking at the pics.

Amari woke up extra early this Tuesday morning. He was super excited to show off his new shoes. Amari was feeling good and imagined how he could shut Cardy up for good. After he brushed his teeth, he practiced in the mirror what he was going to say. "These are the Jumps! They just came out. Y'all don't know about these yet."

Amari starts walking to the bus stop when he hears Ty, "Wait up, my boy! I see you got on those jeans and hoodie from my brother. They match your shoes perfect! You look like a baller right now." Amari had a big cheese smile on his face and said, "Thanks, bro. These are the Jumps! They ain't even out yet."

Ty, looking a little confused, said, "For real? I ain't never seen or heard of those. Who play in them?"

Amari said, "I don't know, but they look like the J's, so I got them. Rate my shoes, bro."

Ty used a juggling motion with his hands, nodded, and said, "6-7! Ha! But it don't matter, bro…They clean. You look straight, player."

For a moment, Amari felt confident. But before the bus even stopped for him, he could hear Cardy's voice. Once the bus door opened, he knew it would be a long ride.

"Ok! I see you, Amari. You got on them fresh kicks. Walking like a duck. You scared to get a crease in your shoes?" Cardy sarcastically and loudly yelled from the back of the bus. Amari's moment had arrived. He practiced in the mirror earlier, and he was ready. He said, "These are the Jumps. They just came out. Y'all don't know about these yet!" Feeling triumphant and confident, Amari, with his head up, strutted to his seat like the number 1 pick in the NBA draft, then sat down.

Cardy had a devilish grin and loudly shouted out, "The Jumps? BAAAAAAAHHHHH!!! I ain't never heard of them. You need to put them in the dumps!" The kids on the bus erupted in laughter so loud that the bus driver screamed to everyone, "Shut up and stay in your seats! It's a railroad crossing!"

Once the bus quieted down, Cardy yelled out one last crack. "You should've got the J's, my boy. Those is trash! Rated zero, bro."

Everybody laughed again, and Amari's feelings were hurt. "Shut up, Cardy, you doing too much," Ty said. Then he looked at Amari and said, "Don't worry about her. You still fresh!" Amari looked concerned and thought to himself, "Maybe I should have gotten something else or just waited until Friday."

Chapter 5: The Cost of Confidence

Once Amari got to school, he walked with his feet at a 45-degree angle and wouldn't bend his knees. People kept asking him why he was walking like that. Amari said, "I just got new shoes, and I don't want to crease them." Amari was walking down the hall, heading to recess, when he heard a pleasant, soft voice coming from behind him. It was his crush, Isabella!

"Hey, nice shoes," Isabella said, with a smile. Amari responded with a confident smirk on his face, having practiced in the mirror that morning. He replied, "These are the Jumps. They just came out. Y'all don't know about these yet."

With a grand smile on her face, Isabella said, "Boy… Just say thanks. I don't care about that. Sometimes you be doing too much... Anyway, are you going to play basketball at recess? We're going to practice cheerleading when y'all play. I hope you get all the points!"

Amari didn't want to mess up his shoes on his first day wearing them, but he wanted to show off for Isabella. Amari was grinning from ear to ear and said, "I wasn't going to, but I will if y'all gonna cheer."

As they approached the basketball courts, he heard a loud voice. "Come on, Amari! We need you on our team!" Ty called out. Amari walked out for recess but hesitated. He looked at the ground and saw rocks, puddles, and dirt. He didn't want to mess up his new shoes. But he also wanted to play for Isabella and the other cheerleaders.

Ty excitedly yelled out and said, "I got Amari! He on my team!" Amari proudly walked over to Ty and bent over to tighten up his shoelaces. Amari couldn't worry about his shoes anymore. Isabella was way more important. It's showtime!

The game started, and Amari played like a star. He kept looking over at Isabella and the cheerleaders to make sure they saw him score. Amari showed off his hezy-crossover and step back jumper. "Kobe!" he screamed as he let the ball go. He scored! The teachers blew the whistle, and there was no more time for another game. All the cheerleaders were jumping and clapping. The other students came up to him, saying how great that shot was. Amari is feeling good again!

After all the excitement ended, Amari looked down at his shoes in shock and thought to himself, "Dang-uh!!!" His brand-new Jumps already had a crease on the top of both shoes. They were dirty and starting to rip on the sides. Amari couldn't believe it! Then he remembered what Blake told him at the shoe store about the quality of the Jumps. Amari started questioning his decision to himself: "Maybe I should have got those Iversons or just waited until Friday."

After recess, it was time for school to end. Amari felt a mix of sadness and anger. He wanted to go to the bathroom to wipe them off, but there were no more bathroom breaks for the day. He couldn't show off his new shoes because they looked like old ones now. When the teachers told the bus riders to line up at the door, Amari waited to get in the back of the line. He dreaded getting on the bus with his shoes ripped and dirty.

Chapter 6: Sacrifice for Glory

Ty and Amari sat together on the ride home. Ty leaned over with his fist pointed at Amari for a fist bump, then said, "You was killing them boys, today with that jump shot. You're really getting good, bro."

Amari hit the fist bump with an explosion and said, "Thanks! But look at my shoes. They all messed up. I just hope Cardy don't start on me, bro."

"Forget her! She can't play ball like you or cheer. Did you know… They say she's 13 and can barely even read… and she's in the 4th grade!" Ty exclaimed.

For most of the bus ride home, Cardy was focusing on somebody else. Amari stayed quiet in his seat, hoping not to bring attention to himself. But right before his stop, Cardy yelled out and laughingly said,

"YO! Amari, what happened to your Jumps? I told you they belong in the dumps!" The kids on the bus were laughing and pointing just like before. One kid fell out of the seat laughing. It looked like someone knocked him over with a shot from a paintball.

Amari stood up like an oak tree and boldly responded, "Leave me alone! At least I can read!" The students on the bus began looking at Cardy and laughing, then said, "Ooooooooh..." Now the negative attention has shifted in the opposite direction. Some of the students started calling her "lame" and "retarded." Some kids pulled out papers and books from their backpacks, shoving them in Cardy's face, saying, "Read this... You really can't read?" Cardy abruptly stopped talking, sat down, and started crying.

Amari was high-fiving Ty and the others around him. But when he looked back before getting off the bus, he saw her sitting quietly with her head down. Amari knew he needed to stand up for himself, but he felt bad about it.

Ty was laughing and said, "You finally got her! I bet she'll leave you alone from now on."

Amari looked at Ty with a non-confident look, saying, "I don't know, bro. Look at my shoes, they really are trash. I should've waited or got something else. My mom is going to kill me!"

Chapter 7: Patience is a Virtue

Amari went into the house and ran up the stairs as quickly as he could. He wanted to wipe off his shoes before his mom got home. He turned on the water in the bathroom sink, grabbed his wash rag from earlier, got it wet and soapy, and started scrubbing. He used most of the soap and even tried toothpaste. Nothing was working as he thought. Amari said, "Dang! They won't get clean. I can't get this dirt out. This is some bull…" But before he could finish his curse word, he heard the door open.

"I'm home! Amari. You here?" said his mother, Sharman.

"Yes. I'm upstairs. I'm coming down." Amari frantically wiped off the sink and shoved the dirty rag to the bottom of the clothes basket. Terrified to show his mom what happened, he went downstairs to talk to his mother barefoot.

"Go get those groceries off the steps. I been walking with all these heavy bags from the bus stop and I'm tired." Sharman said. She looked down and noticed Amari was barefoot. "Boy! Get your shoes on first.

Don't you go outside with no shoes on!"

Amari ran back up to get his shoes, but he was scared to come back down. He ran down as fast as he could and grabbed the bags off the step. But surprisingly, Sharman didn't say anything about the shoes. Amari was shocked.

"Thanks, son. How was your day? Did your friends like your shoes?" Mom said.

Amari was trembling in fear. He took one large swallow, *GULP,* and then said, "Not really. Look at them." Sharman looks down and starts dying with laughter, like she's at a comedy show! She's laughing so hard she starts to cry. Surprisingly, and with a big smile, mom says, "Was it worth it? You begged me for shoes yesterday. How do you feel now?"

"Not good. But I really wanted new shoes." Amari said. With a confused and disappointed tone, he continued, "Why you laughing at me?"

"Son. I'm laughing because I did the same thing as you when I was your age. I wanted something so bad, I made poor choices. Next time, you'll listen to your mom and just wait. That way you can get exactly what you want." Sharman reached out with open arms for Amari and hugged him tightly. "I love you, son, and I'm glad you learned your lesson. Have some patience next time."

Amari first thought to himself, "Patience must mean waiting," then said aloud, "You're right, Mom. I thought you was going to be mad. So, can I get those J's on Friday?"

Laughing even louder than before, Sharman walked to the kitchen like she does every day after work. She pulled the lighter and half-smoked, little brown cigar from her pocket, grabbed the bottle from the top of the refrigerator, and poured it into her favorite coffee mug. As she was walking to the bathroom, she took one sip and said, "Boy, bye! You made your choice, now you have to live with it.

Did you know: "*The proportion of expenditures on transportation in the US is often inversely correlated with income. While the average American across all income levels spends roughly* 16% of their household expenditures *on transportation, these costs are not comparable across income brackets. Lower-income households generally pay a* larger portion of their budgets *on transportation and, as people move up in income brackets, they pay less…Low-income communities of color are, as a result,* disproportionately affected *by a lack of access to reliable and accessible public transit services. This leads to many households in these communities having fewer financial resources and time to spend* *on other areas like education, housing, childcare, and healthcare because of the costs of private vehicle ownership. Those that go without cars are often limited in economic and employment opportunities the further they live from urban cores."*

Institute for Transportation and Development Policy, The High Cost of Transportation in the United States, January 24, 2024

General Discussion:

1. How vital are nonverbal cues in this story? Identify a few, then interpret.
2. At what point do you think kids know what their parents are doing "behind closed doors"? How can a parent tell?
3. Did you feel sorry for anyone in this story? Why? How would you coach them?
4. How can you identify a student/person struggling with emotional control? What behaviors do they display?
5. What characters acted out? How? Why?

Questions posed by Dr. Sonya Berle, DSW, LICSW, CADAC IV, ASID Associate.

Cultural and Clinical Processing

1. Mr. Kersey quotes Dr. Kenneth Hardy's term "Cultural Camouflage" before the story begins. If you consider the cultural camouflage to be clinical defenses at work, which defenses can you identify in this story?

2. A theme emerges of leaders and followers. From a human developmental standpoint, why do you think some of the students laugh along with Cardy, and why are they afraid of going against her at this point?

3. Adults can punish the "bully" for their behaviors towards others. What reparative steps and underlying clinical considerations and resources might help adults in communicating with a bullying student, beyond "forced" verbal and written apology notes created by the student?

4. When pondering resiliency, what personality attributes or environmental buffers does Amari have that contribute to his ability to endure the bullying he receives?

Public Health and Structural Thinking

1. Do you see themes of humans helping each other in this story when systemic structures and systems are

failing? If so, who, and please describe the situation.

2. What public health issues are present for Amari's mom, Sharman? What role do you think mirroring and modeling might have in Amari's future as he receives action steps of care and love from mom, while substance use is normalized? What role do you speculate systems/structural oppression play in mom's substance use?

3. Please identify at least three aspects of systemic oppression or poverty barriers you read in this story.

Can you see that?

Chapter 1: Cardy's Secret

Meanwhile, Cardy slumped over in her seat, her eyes welling up with tears. She was humbled and quiet. She finally got exposed by Amari. Cardy felt bad about how she treated people, and she didn't even know why she acted this way. Something was going on, and she couldn't figure it out. All the other stops were complete, and Cardy is the last stop. The bus driver, Ms. Karen, says, "You'll be ok. But you can't mistreat people and expect good things to happen to you. You're never like this. Is there something wrong?"

While patting and scratching her head, Cardy replied, "My head has been itching a lot at the end of the day, but I don't know why."

"Well, go home, wash it, and you'll probably be ok." The bus driver said. "Hey, before you go, will you check the emergency row and make sure nothing is there?"

Cardy paused in the middle of the aisle in a frightened state. She was a deer in the headlights. "Which one is that?" she asked.

Ms. Karen, sitting in her seat, looked up at Cardy through the mirror and replied with a frustrated tone.

"Can't you read? It says EMERGENCY!"

"Not good. I can read some stuff, but I gotta get real close or just guess." Cardy said, with her eyes tearing up again. She was embarrassed.

Ms. Karen said very lovingly, but with a concerned tone, "Dang…I'm sorry, baby. I didn't mean to make you feel bad. I just thought the kids were teasing. I didn't know it was that deep. Well… just hand me the folder out of seat 23, so I can do my bus check after you leave."

"I know my numbers, though. That's easy!" Cardy said as she wiped her eyes and bolted to the seat. She grabbed the folder. "Here you go!"

As Ms. Karen grabbed the folder, she said, "Thanks, baby…hey…wait a minute. This is from seat 32! Never mind… is your momma home?" Ms. Karen was becoming increasingly inquisitive and growing more concerned.

"Yeah…but am I in trouble?" Cardy fearfully asked.

"No, but I need to talk to her about this. I think I can help." She said with a smile. What's your mom's name?

"Jasmine," Cardy said.

Ms. Karen pulls the bus over to the side of the road

and turns on the blinking hazard lights. As they walked to the apartment, Cardy didn't know what was going on. No one has ever cared if she could read, see, or even try to help her. Ms. Karen discussed her son's struggles with his eyesight and schoolwork with Cardy and how he eventually received the help he needed. Ms. Karen proudly talked about how he gets straight A's and is on his way to Ball State University to be a teacher.

Chapter 2: What the…?

As they got closer to her building, a small group of guys were hanging out outside, as they do every day. Cardy began to get nervous and started walking fast. She could no longer focus on what Ms. Karen was saying because she was watching to see what these older boys were going to do.

"Hey, fine shit! Looking good."

"Look at that booty!"

"Come over here and talk to me real quick."

"Yo! Cardy! Come here!"

A group of young people, including middle- and high-school-aged boys, was hanging outside the apartment building near Cardy's residence. Some were drinking beer, some vaping, others yelling and harassing her, as they do daily.

"Come on, Ms. Karen, RUN! That's what I do every day after school when I'm coming home." Cardy said.

"Wait, what? I ain't running nowhere…" Ms. Karen stood tall, with her fists balled up, and angrily yelled at the group. "HEY!!! Leave us alone, or I'm calling the police on y'all! This little girl is in the 4th grade! Y'all too old to be messing with her! If I see y'all when I drop her off tomorrow, you better let her pass, or you're going to deal with me! Do y'all understand?

"Yes, ma'am! We sorry. We was just joking around." The oldest boy, Kevin, yelled back.

While walking to the apartment, Ms. Karen just kept going on and on about her son and how much trouble he was for her when he was Cardy's age. She talked about him fighting all the time and never listening to his teachers. She discussed how he would get frustrated, tear up his room, and just cry. Ms. Karen continued talking about how helpless she felt because she didn't know how to help her son. She explained in depth, saying, "Mr. Brandon worked with him and got him tested for learning disabilities. I finally found out he had dyslexia. Cardy, do you know what that means?"

Cardy was rolling her eyes and looking up at the sky,

hoping she would just shut up. "Huh? What you say? My bad. I wasn't listening."

Ms. Karen sighed and said, "Never mind…"

Cardy was thinking about being in trouble, feeling anxious, and somewhat nervous about Ms. Karen going to her apartment. She started walking slowly and started making excuses. "My mom might not be there. I'll just tell her you came by."

"No. I need to talk to your mom. She needs to know what's going on so I can help you. You're not in trouble, so don't worry. What is your address?" Ms. Karen said.

Cardy, looking confused and bothered, said, "I don't know. I know it's right down this street at the end. Ain't no number on the door."

Knock! Knock! Knock! Ms. Karen politely knocked on the door. "Watch out, Ms. Karen…" Cardy stated as she walked through the unlocked door. "She know I'm coming, so the door be open after school… MOMMA???? MOMMA!!!! MS. KAREN HERE TO TALK TO YOU! … Hold up right here, Ms. Karen. I'll go up to her room and get her real quick." Ms. Karen waited patiently at the door, cautiously looking around the living room. She saw "the guy on the couch." A man was sleeping on the couch, surrounded by empty beer bottles, a box of Newport cigarettes, and a PS5 controller on the table. Ms. Karen was looking up, silently praying to God, "Please Lord, don't let this man wake up while I'm here…" and hoping the guy on the couch would stay sleeping.

With a bright smile and a welcoming vibe, Ms. Karen said, "Hello! I'm Karen. I drive the school bus. I wanted to tell you about Cardy real quick, if that's cool."

Cardy's mom comes strolling downstairs, tired and just waking up. Her reddish colored eyes are barely open. She is wearing a shiny green bonnet with "GUCCI" in bright pink letters, holding a half-lit cigarette and a watered-down drink in the same hand, and tightly covering herself in a pink silk robe.

With a surprised and happy look, Ms. Karen said, "Wow! Cardy, why didn't you tell me your mom is an A-K-A?"

Cardy and Jasmine, in unison, with confused looks, said, "What's an A-K-A?"

Chapter 3: Death of the killer weave

Ms. Karen said, "My bad, never mind… anyway…Hello!"

Mom said, "Hey girl, I'm Jasmine. Cardy knows I be sleep 'til she gets out of school. What she do? She's never in any trouble, but I been getting voicemails from the school since yesterday. I work nights, and I'm usually sleep."

Jasmine rubbed her eyes to make sure she was seeing clearly. After she walked down the last steps, she knew she was seeing everything just fine. "What the…? What is that on your head?" Jasmine, with anger in her eyes and somewhat perplexed, reached over and snatched Cardy by the hair. "What the hell is this? Where you get this weave from? Oh, you think you grown? I'm ready to beat yo … ooooooo, I ain't got time for this today. I'm throwing this thang in the trash outside."

Cardy was terrified and confused, saying, "Huh? I don't know. I was telling Ms. Karen that my head was itching since yesterday. What is it?"

"It's a damn weave, girl. You know what it is. Is this why you been acting up in school and on the bus? You trying to be a baddie?" Jasmine said.

Finally, the spell was broken! Cardy was starting to have a better attitude and even smiling. She was still a little foggy and confused when she said, "I don't remember that. I was feeling a little crazy, but I feel good again now. Thanks, Momma. I love you." Cardy hugged her mom with all her might.

Ms. Karen was so happy for them that she was

almost crying. "I'm so happy we got that situation in order. But that's not why I came. I noticed that Cardy is having trouble seeing the signs and numbers on the bus. Has she been tested?"

Jasmine seemed to take offense at her comments. She looked her up and down from head to toe and said, "What you mean tested? Ain't nothing wrong with my baby!"

Ms. Karen went on to explain the earlier situation to make Jasmine aware of Cardy's possible condition. Ms. Karen was understanding about Jasmine's attitude and stated, "I'm not trying to insult you or Cardy. She's a good kid. I just noticed a few things today and wanted to make you aware. I'll get out of your way." Ms. Karen back pedaled her way out of the door.

Jasmine said, "I got this. You just worry about driving that bus!" Then slammed the door in her face. "What that lady mean you can't see and don't know your words? You can read, can't you?"

Cardy said in a reluctant, fearful, and low tone. "Sometimes it's blurry if I'm not close up to it or I just don't know the words, so I guess sometimes."

Jasmine, still fuming, snatched Cardy's book bag off the floor and grabbed the first book she saw. She opened it in the middle of the book and said, "Here!

Read page 105."

Cardy said, "The words are too small. Can I hold it?" Cardy holds the book so close to her face, it's almost touching her nose, and she starts to read, "The… poll lives by …uh… glasses in the water…because of the clim…um… frig water…uh…Is that right?"

With a negative and frustrated attitude, Jasmine yelled, "Girl, gimme that book." As she looked at the text, she was instantly shocked and concerned. She started to realize her child may have a serious problem, and she had no clue. "Dang girl, it say, 'The polar bear lives by glaciers in the water because of the climate.' Now turn to 76 and try to read that." Jasmine stood over her, arms crossed, growing increasingly angry. "Hurry up!!"

Cardy turned to what she thought was page 76, but it was really page 67. Jasmine's eyes began to water, then tears ran down her face. She was very sad for Cardy and angry with herself. "I'm sorry, Cardy. That's my bad. I didn't know. I work so much that I thought everything was going good in school. You've been getting B's and C's on your report card for years now... We going to Walgreens to get you some glasses real quick. At least you'll be able to see tomorrow."

Chapter 4: This some bull…

Once Jasmine and Cardy arrived at Walgreens, Jasmine said, "We finna get your eyes checked real quick and get you some glasses." Cardy looked at her mom with relief and admiration. Cardy felt loved and was glad her mom was paying attention to her.

"Thanks for bringing me, Mom. I love you!" Cardy said with a big smile on her face.

Jasmine was holding Cardy's hand and looking for the nearest person with a Walgreens name badge. She spotted a girl near a counter. She was wearing a red smock with a crooked name tag that said, "BONQUESHA." The cashier had 2-inch multicolored fingernails with fake diamonds. Her eyelashes looked like black fans stuck to her eyeballs, wearing a long, blonde, red, and purple streaked weave that went past her butt, a hand on her hip, bad attitude, popping her bubble gum, using a nasty, disrespectful tone, not even looking up to address Jasmine, while scrolling on her phone said "What you need?"

Jasmine, already frustrated, looked at the cashier, ready to curse her out. But Cardy was smiling and squeezing her mom's hand. Jasmine looked down and reminded herself to be a good role model for her daughter. She used one of her favorite coping skills.

Jasmine closed her eyes, took a deep breath, and politely said, "Where do we get glasses from?"

"You got a prescription? If you ain't got no prescription, you can look over there. They got some on that rack that spins around. All the different prescriptions are over there, but they some ugly glasses." Bonquesha said, while pointing to the rack with the long, diamond-studded index finger, twirling the purple streak in her weave, and still gazing into her phone.

"Where I get a subscription from?" Jasmine very curiously stated.

"Ha… you mean prescription? Duh… the eye doctor." The cashier said, then smirked, as she rolled her eyes and returned to scrolling on her phone.

"Come on, girl. Let's look on this rack." Jasmine was embarrassed but proceeded to the rack to see if any of the glasses would work for Cardy. She quietly said, "We're going to have to look through all these and see which ones you can see out of… These are just for now. I'm going to get you an appointment with the eye doctor as soon as I get home."

Cardy and Mom looked and looked through all the glasses. Jasmine started spinning the rack round and around. There were big green ones, little red ones, and some even had chains hanging from the sides, perfect for an old lady. Some were too big, others too small, and finally, after trying on at least 15 pairs, she found a pair that fit perfectly. Jasmine said, "Hey! Those look good. They look like they fit. If you can see out of these, I think we can get those if they take this Medicaid card. Can you see that sign?"

Cardy looked up. Her big brown eyes filled the lenses, as if she were looking out of the bottom of an old soda bottle. She said, "Yeah, Momma, I can see. It say, 'Free Flu Shot', Is that right?"

Jasmine was relieved and finally exhaled. "Ahhh. About time. We good then. Let's go."

"These are ugly! They finna be laughing at me at school tomorrow. Can't I just wait until we go to the eye doctor? Please!?" Cardy said in a disappointing tone. Her face was a picture of sadness. She imagined her bus ride to school, wondering how Amari or Ty would tease her.

"Lil girl. Learn to be grateful. This is the best I can do right now… How much are these? Oh. It says $18.99. Let's get out of here and get back home. I still gotta work tonight." Jasmine said as she anxiously and briskly walked to the cashier with her Medicaid card. She was hoping she could get the glasses for free.

With poor customer service, the cashier, Bonquesha,

was having a conversation on her AirPods, and she loudly said, "Girl, hold on real quick. I gotta help this lady… It'll be $20.32. But you can't use that Medicaid card. That'll be for your eye doctor when you set up the appointment. Then you can get the free glasses." Bonquesha continued with the same nasty, mean tone and attitude. "You want them or not? It's other people in line."

"This is some bull…" Jasmine expressed in a disappointing and quiet voice, then stated, "We'll just come back. I don't have no money on me."

As she began to walk away, disappointed and embarrassed, she heard a deep voice say, "I got you, miss lady. I'll pay for it." She turned around and saw Superman! He was a tall, athletically built, well-groomed, wavy-haired, dark-skinned man. Jasmine looked up at him a little longer than usual. She was in awe. She saw he was wearing a badge but couldn't see the name very well. She couldn't help but think how handsome this man is. Jasmine's frowns finally turned into a smile. As the gentleman swiped his Titanium American Express Card, he said with a smile, "Don't worry, sista, I got it. Have a good day."

Jasmine said, " Thank you," and started to cry. "No one ever helps us. I appreciate you!"

Cardy jokingly said with a big grin, "Dang Momma!

You crushin' on him. That's Mr. Brandon. He works at our school. He always helps us and gives us food and stuff. You should marry him!" Cardy started to laugh.

"Shut up, little girl, and come on... Let's go." Jasmine said while wiping away her tears and smiling. "So, he works at the school? Hmmm…I gotta come up there anyway."

Chapter 5: My bad…

The next day (Wednesday), Jasmine was very tired, having just got home from her shift at the warehouse. She usually goes to bed, but she felt bad about the day before. She wanted to ensure Cardy felt supported and thanked Ms. Karen for looking out for her daughter. On her way home, Jasmine bought a breakfast sandwich from the gas station. As she walked into the house, she quietly passed the guy on the couch and put it on the table. She tiptoed up the stairs to Cardy's room, shook her gently, and whispered, "Wake up, girl! I got you a sandwich. After you get dressed and eat, come get me. I need to walk you to the bus and talk to Ms. Karen."

Barely awake, with sleep in her eyes, Cardy said, "Ok, momma. Am I still in trouble?"

"Naw. You good. Just hurry up. I want to get back home so I can get some sleep." Jasmine said.

When the school bus pulled up, and the door opened, Ms. Karen looked shocked and said, "Oh, hey girl. How are you doing this morning?"

Jasmine, holding her hands like she was praying, humbly said, "I'm so sorry about yesterday. I shouldn't have talked to you like that—my bad, girl. I was just waking up and having a bad day. We cool?"

Ms. Karen smiled and said, "Don't worry about it, girl. People have good and bad days all the time. Thanks for apologizing, though. What did you decide to do about Cardy?"

Jasmine exhaled heavily and said, "Girl, I called about an eye appointment, but she can't get in for 2 weeks. We bought some glasses at Walgreens, but she really don't like how they look. I doubt if she even wears them today."

Cardy walks up the steps and gets on the bus. While closing the bus door, Ms. Karen said, "We gotta go, for I make these kids late. I'll make sure she has them on when she gets off the bus. Oh, and by the way, go up to the school and talk to Mr. Brandon. He's the school social worker. He can get things done really fast and help with any testing she might need."

Jasmine lit up with a smile! "Mr. Brandon? I'm going up to the school after I go home and get dressed."

Cardy watched her mother apologize, and she felt she needed to do the same when Amari got on the bus. When the bus stopped for Amari and Ty, Cardy took her glasses off, stood up, and smiled. Amari stopped in his tracks, shocked, but he kept walking toward the back of the bus.

Ty nudged Amari in the back and whispered, "Don't pay her no attention, bro. She's just gonna get you mad again."

With a bright smile and a nervous tone, Cardy said, "Amari, I'm sorry. I was mean to you, and that's not fair. Can we be cool again?"

Amari lit up with happiness and excitement. "Sure! Can I sit by you?"

With a confused look, Ty shook his head "no" and said, "Bro, you a simp."

Cardy was still smiling and began to smirk. With a laughing voice, Cardy said, "Yes. And I got something to show you but promise you won't laugh." Cardy reluctantly but playfully pulled her new glasses out of her pocket. "Promise you won't laugh and close your eyes."

Amari saw the glasses in her hand and was already laughing. He was holding his stomach like Santa. "Ok, Ok, Ok, I won't laugh." Amari closed his eyes and covered his mouth. When he opened his eyes, they teared up. Amari started laughing so hard he could barely breathe. When he finally calmed down, he said, "You kinda look like Luke in those glasses. He looks funny as hell in his, but you don't. You look cool. It was just funny to me to see you with glasses."

Cardy snatched those glasses off her face as fast as she could. She turned toward Amari, with a bad attitude and a finger pointed toward the sky, she said, "Wait a minute. Who is Luke?"

Chapter 6: Luke loves Candy

"Luke is the smartest boy in our class. He always answers all the questions, and he's the teacher's pet. He used to help me with my reading and math work. You should talk to him." Amari stated. "He always sits by himself at breakfast and lunch, too. I'll show you when we get to school."

With her face wrinkled and lips scrunched up, Cardy said, "You mean the white boy?"

Luke is a great kid who has been living with his aunt and uncle since kindergarten. Ironically, his apartment is one block over from Cardy's. His uncle takes him to school because his uncle works the first shift at the warehouse and doesn't want Luke getting into fights or bullied at the bus stop. He is shorter than most of the kids in 4th grade, but he loves to read and play chess. He doesn't have many friends, but that's not because of a lack of effort. Luke has been trying to make friends, but they treat him poorly because he's different. He's not very good at basketball, football, or soccer. He doesn't run very fast, but he can read high school-level books. He's very good with technology, and he's completed all his math homework for the year in 2 months!

Luke has learned to avoid trouble by sitting alone at breakfast. Luke keeps his head in his books while he eats and doesn't bother anyone.

Amari walks up, speaking loudly, "Luke… Yo Luke! This Cardy. She's my friend, and she needs some help with her work. Can you help her?"

Luke was somewhat confused and looking up through thick lenses with those big brown eyes, and said, "Hi! I can help. I know all that stuff already." Luke was happy someone was talking to him and told Cardy, "You can sit here if you want. Do you like candy? Y'all want some?"

Luke unzipped his backpack, and it looked like a candy store! There were all kinds of snacks and a few toys inside.

"Hell yeah!"

"Me too!"

"I want that KitKat!"

"Let me get that Reese cup!"

Amari, Ty, Cardy, and some random 5th graders all yelled out something to get a piece of candy from Luke.

Amari said, "Oooo! Let me get that toy car! I love those…"

Luke said, "OK. But don't play with it in school. I don't want people to know." Amari abruptly interrupted and said, "I know. I know. I ain't gone tell nobody."

Cardy said, "Thanks for the candy. Oh yeah... I just got these new glasses. I couldn't see the words on the board, but now I can. Oh, and I ain't good with math either."

As the bell rang, they got up and headed to class. Luke said, "When we get to math, I'll ask Mr. Yung if I can sit by you and help."

As the students heard the first bell, they began leaving the cafeteria and heading down the hall to class. Random kids kept coming up to Luke and saying, "Let me get some candy! We heard you got that good in there."

Luke was smiling from ear to ear. He was so happy

that people were talking to him. He thought he was making lots of new friends. He unzipped his backpack to check his stash, and it was still full of all kinds of candy. He said to himself, "I'm still good on candy until tomorrow for sure."

Perplexed, Cardy said, "That's a lot of candy you're giving out. Are all these kids your friends? Do you do this every day?"

"Yeah! I got lots of friends. I'm cool with all of them… and no, not every day. I just got a lot yesterday and wanted to bring it to school." Luke said as they were walking into the classroom. "Hey, Mr. Yung. Can I sit by Cardy today and help her with her work?"

Chapter 7: Math sucks

"Quiet down, quiet down…everybody get in their seats, open up your computers and get on Dream Box." said Mr. Yung. All the students scrambled toward their seats and dug through their desks for their laptops.

"You guys should be on lesson 12 by now. If not, you need to do your past assignments first. Hey Luke, since you're finished with your work, will you help the others get on the right lessons?"

"But Mr. Yung, I was going to help Cardy today. You

said I could sit by her to help. Remember?" Luke said.

"Huh? I didn't say that. But if Cardy needs help, she can ask." My Yung replied. "Cardy…Cardy! Do you really want help today? Hey…wait a minute. You got new glasses…I like those. Come sit by Luke and finish all those assignments you've missed over the last 2 days."

In between the lessons, Cardy is getting comfortable enough to tell Luke what's going on in her life, and Luke is doing the same. Luke is showing her ways to do math and how to sound out words. They are quietly talking and becoming friends.

Mr. Yung is constantly exhausted. He gives his best effort, but, per Indiana Department of Education standards, Principal Preston requires all teachers to explain the district's concepts and strategies for solving even the simplest math problems. He continues to try to walk around and help every student he can, but there is never enough time. Most of the students in the school were Black Americans. Over the last five years, the student body has seen an increase in students of Latin descent, alongside a growing number of Haitian students. Some of the students only speak Haitian Creole or Spanish. They have either an ENL assistant for an hour per day or a class partner. Some are bilingual, and others know only their native language. Most immigrant students continue to struggle with comprehending the lessons.

"Jorge, comprendo?" Mr. Yung says, looking at the stressed and confused expression on his student's face.

As the Spanish-speaking children laugh, Maritza says, "Mr. Yung. You have to say…' "Jorge ¿entiendes?"

"Oh…my bad. I'm still trying to learn a little Spanish. Thanks for correcting me. Will you help Jorge? He looks lost." Mr. Yung said, smiling.

"I got it, Mr. Yung…Lo entiendo Señor Yung." Maritza says with a big smile.

After he worked his way around the room, answering as many questions as he could, he spent the last 15 minutes at the board, helping the 4th graders with double-digit multiplication problems. They have been working on this for weeks, and lots of them still don't get it, but Mr. Yung has to move on to the next lesson. "Keep trying, guys. I know it's hard. Ask your parents for help or try searching YouTube for multiplication lessons. I'm sorry, but we have to move on. It'll be a new lesson tomorrow, so try to get some help at home... It's time for recess and lunch. Everybody, go LINE UP!"

In a disappointed tone, you could hear a collective

"*awwww*" as lots of the kids complained and became more depressed. Amari speaking out said, "Aw, man. This is too hard, and my momma said she can't help me with the new math, and our Wi-Fi don't be working all the time. I just can't do it." Other kids joined in, disgusted and commenting…

"I just don't care no more. I ain't never gonna get it anyway." Said Kyrie with his palm on his forehead.

"My mom don't even know English, bro. I'm just gonna work construction with my dad when I get older anyway. He lets me work with him now on the weekends." Jorge said while hitting the desk with his pencil.

Marcellus was rubbing his eyes and said, "I was sleep. What happened?"

"I'm just ready for recess and lunch. I'm hungry." Korbyn said while his stomach growled.

All the students are still playing around while trying to get in line order. Meanwhile, the classroom becomes increasingly louder. Mr. Yung starts to sweat in frustration, eyes watering with empathy, and rubbing his head in disgust, yells, "HEY!!! LINE UP! LEVEL ZERO VOICES! I don't understand y'all sometimes. Everyone is always playing around, and you don't know your math facts! This is serious business! I only get to teach you math for 45 minutes a day. You all have to lock in and pay attention. Did you know that at this school, only 13% of you passed the ILEARN test last year? That's a little more than 1 out of every 10 students. And quiet as it's kept, only 8% of y'all passed IREAD last year. That's a little less than 1 out of 10 of y'all can read at or above your grade level. Y'all need to stop playing so much and get serious about your schoolwork. No one cares about our school or this neighborhood. If you don't want to be poor for the rest of your life, you gotta get your reading and math facts! Y'all are gonna have to find a way to work together or use TikTok for math, or somethin'. Y'all use it to do those stupid dances every day. Do your math facts!"

Did you know: *"Dyslexia is thought to be one of the most common language-based learning disabilities. It is the most common cause of reading, writing, and spelling difficulties. Of people with reading difficulties, 70–80% are likely to have some form of dyslexia. It is estimated that between 5–10% of the population has dyslexia, but this number can also be as high as 17%. The symptoms of dyslexia range from mild to severe. Because dyslexia may not be recognized and diagnosed in some individuals, they do not receive the necessary treatment; others may not disclose that they are diagnosed. These mitigating factors make the prevalence of dyslexia difficult to precisely determine."*

University of Michigan: How many people are

affected by dyslexia? How common is it?
dyslexiahelp.umich.edu

General Discussion:

1. How would you coach a teacher who is dealing with this type of class environment? What skills would you introduce?
2. How much responsibility does the school hold for discovering diagnostic problems in students?
3. What underlying factors could be a result of youth stealing?
4. What are effective ways to coach or teach children with low literacy rates or poor comprehension skills?
5. What advice would you give working parents (caregivers) with low literacy rates, on how to stay involved and educated in their child's education? Health? Practical steps only.

Questions posed by Dr. Sonya Berle, DSW, LICSW, CADAC IV, ASID

Cultural and Clinical Processing

1. As clinicians and educators, delivering information to caregivers can raise unanticipated emotions in the receiver. As a clinician or educator, what is the best practice method to deliver potentially sensitive or negative news to a caregiver? Second, when we

receive unexpected anger from a caregiver, how can we best de-escalate the situation? How can we then process the exchange after the fact, so we do not hold another's anger or surprise?

2. After receiving strong reactions, as the bus driver, Ms. Karen, did from Jasmine (Cardy's mom), how can we know if we are balancing QTIP (Quick Taking It Personally) with self-reflection for our own blind spots and growth areas?

3. Clinically, what role did shame play in Cardy's externalizing behaviors?

4. Clinically, without unveiling Cardy's vision problems, what mental health symptomatology and potential diagnosis was Cardy presenting with? Once we knew of the physiological basis behind behaviors, how did/does that change your assessment?

5. In Chapter Five, what modeling did Cardy learn from her mom and bring to school the next day?

Public Health and Structural Thinking

1. How many of your youth and families struggle with the constraints of Medicaid, lapses, lack of caregiver insurance, and other healthcare barriers? Do you know who, across various organizational domains (schools, hospitals, churches), can help facilitate or advocate for families in your

community?

2. How do you read and see structural barriers and systemic oppression affecting Jasmine's ability to be mindfully present with Cardy? She demonstrates care and action steps for her child, yet does she have extra time? Do you see a theme of a lack of time with caregivers' capacities to be present throughout this book?

3. Do you see a theme of the community having each other's back when systems fail? If so, what about when the community runs out of resources? How different are the resource needs and stressors in this story as compared to your resource needs and stressors?

HOOSIER DADDY?

Chapter 1: Busted and Disgusted

Amari whispered to Korbyn, "Luke got all that candy in his bookbag. Just get some real quick. He ain't looking." Amari pointed at the bag, then Korbyn reached in and took a big handful.

"HEY! That's my bag. Get out of my bag!" Luke yelled and then sprinted toward Korbyn, knocking over others in the process.

"What's going on? Luke, calm down…" Mr. Yung said.

"He was in my bag, stealing. I don't play that shit, bro. Ain't nobody stealing from me." Luke yelled out.

"I just wanted a piece of candy. I was hungry. I'll put it back, but he got so much in there I didn't think he would know it was gone." Korbyn said.

As Mr. Yung took the bag and told them to line back up, he said, "This bag is heavy. How much candy do you have in here, boy?" Mr. Yung opened the backpack, looked in the bag, and told Luke, "We'll talk about this after lunch. I know you didn't buy all this candy. Where did you get it from?"

Luke lined up silently and didn't say another word.

"As a matter of fact, I'm taking both of y'all to the

reset room. I'll let them deal with this. I'm taking this bag too." Mr. Yung said.

"Please no!" Luke said. "I just want to go to recess and lunch. He can have the candy."

As they walk down the hall to the lunchroom. Mr. Yung stops at the reset room #201 to drop off the bag and tell them what happened with Luke and his use of foul language.

After the class went downstairs, Mr. Terrance and Mr. Gomez looked in the bag, only to discover the missing candy from their room. "Hey! Did you see this? That boy stole all our candy. We'll catch him after lunch today. He's going to be in big trouble stealing from us." Mr. Terrance angrily said. He couldn't believe Luke did this!

Mr. Gomez and Mr. Terrance have been working at the school for years. If there are any problems in the classrooms, the teachers will call for one of these men to help the students reset their attitudes or behaviors, then return to class.

Mr. Terrance Famos is a millionaire philanthropist who dedicates his time to teaching and volunteering at churches worldwide. In 1999, he invented a drum machine that the world's top music producers have used. He sold his company for $200 million and donates his salary every year to charity.

Mr. Terrance makes sure there are no problems in the school. He fixes all the computers, monitors the lunch periods, and stays after school for the band and drum line practice. Mr. Gomez is also an essential part of the school. He also works in the lunchroom, serving as a translator, soccer coach, mentor, and running coach.

They have created a school store where kids can earn food, snacks, toys, and shoes by demonstrating good behavior. They host pizza parties for students who achieve perfect attendance or pass their reading and math tests each month. They have backpack giveaways, shoe drives, and assist with school supplies.

Chapter 2: The Black Experience

After lunch, it's time for recess. Luke has a new friend who enjoys talking with him and seems genuinely interested in his thoughts. Cardy invites Luke to join her and her friends at the basketball courts. Luke explains that he sucks at basketball, but he likes to shoot the ball. The boys need an extra player to make the teams even. Cardy tells Amari to let Luke play basketball while she plays like a cheerleader with the other girls. Amari is cool with that. He and the other boys play ball, casually calling each other "nigga" before and during the game. Luke hasn't been getting the ball for most of the game and wanted to participate.

Luke is wide open! He is ready to shoot. Luke has his hands up, jumping up and down, then says, "Hey nigga! Pass me the ball! Nigga, I'm open! Pass it!" Immediately, a loud gasp came from the cheerleaders and other kids watching the game. No one could believe it. *POW! BANG! SMACK! SLAP! BOOM!* Luke was overwhelmed with a barrage of fists and feet flying at him. He covered up in the fetal position, like a roly-poly bug, and said, "Please stop…what did I do? Ok, okay, stop! Stop, please!"

Kyrie, Ernesto, and Amari jumped on Luke and beat him with furious anger, saying, "Don't be calling us no nigga! You can't say that! You a white boy. White people can't say that." Simultaneously, they all heard loud whistles blowing and teachers yelling to stop. The teachers, Mrs. White and Ms. Jackson, ran over to help Cardy break up the fight and investigate the situation. "You boys are always fighting other kids. You're all in trouble now. Go to the door and line up. I'm calling Mr. Brandon and Principal Preston. You're all getting suspended for beating on Luke!"

Ernesto tried to explain. "Wait. But he said…"

"Shut your mouths! I don't care what he said. Tell your story when you get to the office." Mrs. White yelled back. Then the boys started randomly yelling out:

"That's some bullshit!"

"You always take their side because we black."

"That ain't fair. Fuck him!"

"I hate you. You just racist."

The boys are walking toward the office. Amari reaches into his pocket to retrieve the toy Luke gave him earlier that morning. He gets it, takes aim at Luke's head, and with one eye closed, throws the toy car like a major league pitcher at Luke and says, "You a bitch!"

In a strong, deep, loud, and masculine voice, Mr. Yung said, "Amari, that's enough! Hey. Where did you get that car from? Give me that. This looks like mine."

After Amari picked up the toy car off the ground and handed it over, he said, "That's Luke's car. He gave it to me earlier and said I could have it."

In a disappointed tone, Mr. Yung said, "Luke! Please tell me you didn't steal this from my room."

As Mr. Yung picks up Luke and dusts him off, he inspects his injuries. He sees Luke has a busted lip and a few scratches, but nothing serious. "Luke, are you ok? I saw what happened. From where I was, it looked like they started beating on you for no reason. Well… You're alright, lil man... Go with them to the nurse and make sure you're ok, though." Said Mr. Yung.

Cardy and a few teachers console and protect Luke as he walks past the other boys in the office to get to the nurse.

As Cardy and Luke sit in the office, Cardy explains to Luke why his actions are wrong. "Man, bro…you can't be saying that stuff. Them boys beat the brakes off you!" Cardy whispered and laughed. "I'm just joking, but seriously, that's not cool."

Luke replies, "I didn't know. I just wanted to sound cool and be like them. I won't ever do that again."

Chapter 3: American Me

Cardy had her arms in her lap, with her head down, somewhat ashamed. She took a deep breath and said, "I'm going to tell you a secret…My dad is white! My mom told me it was somebody else, but when I'm around my black cousins, they always tease me about it. They told me a long time ago, but I have to act like I don't know, or they'll beat me up for snitching."

"Dang! That's messed up." Luke said while holding an ice pack to the side of his head. "What's the big deal about your white daddy? I'm white too. All this color stuff is stupid. We're all Americans, right?"

Sitting there with her head down, Cardy said, "Not me. They keep telling me I have to say I'm African American. But I ain't never been to Africa before, or my momma either. I'm from Post Road Apartments!"

They both share a laugh until… Mr. Brandon walks up with that deep voice, mean face, and disgusted look. He says, "Hey!!! You think this is funny, Luke? Get to Ms. Preston's office! NOW!!"

The principal, Ms. Preston, calmly called the other boys in the office to get their side of the story and find out what really happened. Upon learning what happened from the boys and Cardy, Mr. Brandon sends them to the reset room with "not so bad" news: they will get in-school suspension instead of being sent home.

"Y'all boys go to room 201. Mr. Terrance and Mr. Gomez will handle it from here. They'll be talking to you about how to handle these types of situations in the future. Y'all just need some coping skills. We'll start working on conflict resolution, communication skills, and even some calm-down steps to help you think before you act. We all have to learn how to control our emotions, no matter what people say." Mr. Brandon said.

Ms. Preston keeps Luke behind to explain what happened, and he tells the truth. He explained that he wanted to fit in and that they kept calling each other nigga, so he thought it was okay. As she explains that it's not, Luke asks a very logical question. "Why can't I say it? All the rappers say it all the time. Everybody in my class says it to each other and laughs about it. They say it in the movies. My uncle even says it when we're driving, and someone cuts in front of us. He calls them a "dumb ass ni…."

"Boy!!! You better not!" Ms. Preston abruptly interrupts. "Now go to 201!"

As Luke starts to walk out, he stops and turns around with a smirk on his face and says, "Real quick, Ms. Preston, I got a question… So, you have to be black to say nigga? That's just stupid!"

Ms. Preston turned fiery red with anger and yelled, "BOY!!!! GET OUT OF HERE AND GO TO 201!"

Chapter 4: Family reunion

Meanwhile, Cardy's mom, Jasmine, received a call from the school asking her to pick up her nephew, Kyrie, for fighting. She gets dressed and hurries to the school.

"I know I'm going to see Mr. Brandon…that chocolate man is handsome!" Jasmine says to herself while looking in the mirror.

After taking off her bonnet, putting on her make-up, fixing her lashes, and changing out of her pink-and-green robe into a nice outfit, she hurries to the school.

While Jasmine approaches the front desk to show her ID to Ms. Carla, Mr. Brandon comes out of his office and says, "So, we meet again? How are you? You're Jasmine, right?"

Jasmine starts to blush and says, "Yes. I'm sorry I look a mess, but I came to get my nephew Kyrie for fighting. Is he ready?"

Mr. Brandon smiles and says, "You look just fine to me! But, since we are trying to keep our suspension numbers down, I'm going to keep him here in the reset room for the remainder of the day. He overreacted to a situation, but we want to help him learn how to manage his emotions in the future. Here. Take my card just in case you need anything. I'll send a letter home with him. I'm sorry you had to come all this way for nothing."

Jasmine, still blushing with a big grin showing off a shiny gold tooth, says, "It's fine… Thank you, and I'll make sure to call you."

As Mr. Brandon goes back to his office, Jasmine

turns around and runs into Luke's uncle. She occasionally sees him at work, but they don't talk much anymore. The secretary at the school, Ms. Carla, knows both of them from when they were younger and says, "Hey! I ain't seen y'all together in a long time." Then she laughingly says, "Are y'all still boyfriend and girlfriend? LOL…everybody knew about y'all." Cardy, Luke, and Kyrie look up at the adults in shock.

"Oooooooooo… Y'all used to be boyfriend and girlfriend?" Cardy and Luke said, while snickering and covering their mouths.

Luke's uncle Bryan said, "Yeah, Luke, that was a long time ago, before I became the Pastor at the church. We broke up before I married your aunt…" Turning to face Jasmine, he said, "Hey, I didn't know you had a daughter? How old is she? She's tall…"

"She's 9, born June 20, 2016," Jasmine said.

"Wow! My birthday is July 20, 2016." Luke said with excitement.

Bryan looks somewhat perplexed at how close they are in age. He begins to look a little harder at Cardy. She is tall, has curly hair, but she is much, much lighter than Jasmine.

Bryan says, "Luke…how do you know her?"

"She's in my class and rides the bus I'm supposed to ride. She lives down the street from us. Just one bus stop over. She's my friend, and I help with her reading and math." Luke said.

Mr. Brandon finally comes back and tells the boys, "Let's go, fellas. Time to go to the reset room." Then he escorts the boys to room 201 and Cardy back to her class.

Chapter 5: Secrets in the Hood

"Hey Jazz…did you and Tony get married?" Uncle Bryan said.

"Don't call me that anymore. And no, Tony went to prison, but he's out now. He's probably still on my couch right now. You think you can get him a job somewhere?"

"Deacon Long and Mr. Julius own a construction company called J&L Construction. They are really good family men who work with older boys at the church, and young men who need a job when they get out of jail. I'll check with them tomorrow and keep you posted… Let me walk you to your car."

"Thanks…whose child is Luke. He called you uncle. You don't even have a brother or sister." Jasmie said.

"You remember Marcy?" Bryan shamefully said.

"The one you left me for. LOL…yes. That's his mom? Where is she?" Jasmine stated with a smirk on her face.

With his eyes watering from sadness, Bryan says, "She's dead, and I've been lying to Luke about it for a while now. He thinks his mom and dad died in a car accident, but the streets took her. After Luke was 2 months old, she left me, and I hadn't seen her in 2 years. So, Marcy's sister stepped up and helped me raise Luke that whole time. We ended up getting married after they found her dead in a ditch by the river. She was beaten up pretty bad, too. They say she had fentanyl in her system and…" Byran couldn't finish the story without crying, so he stopped talking about it.

"Dang. I'm so sorry to hear that. I bet that was tough on you." Jasmine said. "But wait…You married her sister? You know that ain't right, Bryan! But I've got a few secrets I been holding for a while too. Would you like to hear about my life since we broke up?"

After taking a deep breath and wiping the tears from his face, Bryan said, "Yes, of course. I still think about you and wanted to know what happened after us."

"Well…I started dating Tony toward the end of our relationship. After you ghosted me, I found out I was pregnant with Cardy. But after he saw her at the hospital, he wanted a blood test and didn't believe she was his child. So, we took a blood test and found out he was right. He was furious with me! He started breaking things in the house, and then he beat my ass bad. He hurt me and had to go to prison. Anyway…I was only with you before him, so I've been lying too. When Cardy was little, I showed her a picture of 'Drake' and said this was her dad. Then I told Cardy he was in jail for life, and he wanted nothing to do with her. I was drinking a lot and doing drugs back then. I was depressed and just made up a story."

Bryan was in total shock. He couldn't believe what he was hearing. He was shaking his head no, saying, "No way! You're saying that I'm her dad? That's impossible… and who is Drake?"

Chapter 6: Accountability

Bryan and Jasmine exchange phone numbers. While driving home, they had a conversation about the old days and how he acted like he didn't want anything to do with her. So, Jasmine stopped trying to call him after he ignored all her calls and blocked her. Bryan explained that he was a pastor at a church in a neighboring town, had a fiancée, and that his friends had seen them together before. They threatened to tell his congregation and ruin his life. His mother said he wasn't allowed to be with a black woman ever since he was a kid, and the people in his neighborhood threatened to hurt Jasmine if he kept seeing her, so he just went ghost and blocked her.

Jasmine said, "So now what? You're a Pastor and you been lying to that boy all this time? You should be ashamed of yourself. He needs to know the truth, and Cardy does too. We can kill two birds with one stone. Let's take a DNA test and tell the kids what really happened."

"You're right. My congregation won't like it, but it's the only option at this point. God works in mysterious ways, and I'm ready for whatever happens next."

Meanwhile, back at school, Luke was facing serious consequences for lying and stealing. Luke was so embarrassed and ashamed that he just put his head down on a desk and didn't say a word.

"So, you thought it was okay to steal from us?" said Mr. Terrance. "After all the stuff we've given you. Why would you do that? We gave you shoes, backpacks, clothes, extra recess, and everything else. Man, I'm disappointed in you. What do you have to say for yourself?"

With tears rolling down his face, Luke said, "I didn't steal that stuff. I got it from home. That candy was mine. And that car."

“WHAT?” Mr. Gomez said in his outside voice. “So, you’re telling us that all this stuff is yours and you didn’t steal it? Unbelievable Luke. Do you think we are dumb? I’m calling your aunt and letting her know about this. We’re going to get to the bottom of this right now.”

“She ain’t home.” Luke said in a scared tone.

“We’ll see.” Said Mr. Terrance.

Mr. Yung stopped in room 201 on his way back to his class. With a disappointed look and sad tone, he said, “Luke, why did you take that car off my desk? I've been looking for that. It’s not mine, and I was keeping it for another student.”

“I didn’t take it. I swear to God. I found it. I didn’t know it was yours. You can have it back.” Luke said.

“LUKE! Just stop! You got caught, and you’re making it worse. I can’t trust you anymore. You can’t be the class helper and steal from the teacher.” Looking very disappointed and shaking his head no, Mr. Yung said what he said, then walked out of the room.

Everyone is staring at Luke as he cries and pleads for others to believe him. His feelings are hurt, and he doesn’t know what else to do. He puts his head down on the desk and continues to cry.

"BOY! Don't nobody care about them tears. I just got off the phone with your aunt. She said you been bringing all kinds of stuff home, telling her that other kids or teachers are giving it to you. She also said you've been on your computer looking at nasty videos of girls, too. You know what I'm talking about, don't you?... You know what that means?... You can no longer use your laptop in school without supervision, and you can't take it home either. You're lucky school is being dismissed in a few minutes, or I'd make you do some community service to pay it back. I'll see you tomorrow, though. As a matter of fact, you probably stole our Xbox, too." Mr. Terrance casually explained.

Luke looks up, mouth wide open, eyes as big as magnifying glasses, and shaking in fear. Luke knows he's busted. Now he falls out on the floor, crawls under the desk, and cries. All the boys are pointing and laughing at him.

Kyrie said, "HA! That's what you get. Punk ass white boy!"

Luke whispered back while giving him the middle finger, "Fuck you, Kyrie."

Chapter 7: Truth hurts

Luke was terrified to go home. He thought he was in big trouble. Once he got there, he quietly stayed in his room, reading book after book until…

"Hey Luke! Get up! Come on. We need to go to the store, and I want to talk to you." Uncle Bryan said.

Luke puts down his book and quietly walks to the car with his head down. He still doesn't understand why his uncle hasn't said anything about the school incident today. As he rides to the store in silence, he thinks about getting a whippin', being on punishment, doing extra chores, and when he will get his laptop back… His mind is all over the place.

"Luke… hey Luke. Do you hear me? I have something important to tell you… I've made a lot of mistakes in my life, and I understand that people aren't perfect. I'm disappointed in you, but all is forgiven, just like God forgives us of our sins. Can you promise not to do it again?"

Luke looks up in shock and says, "I promise, Uncle Bryan! I will never do that again in my life." Luke begins to crack a smile as his uncle playfully tickles him and roughs up his hair to make him laugh.

"Can I get something from the store? I just want

one thing." Luke said.

"Sure! Hurry up, though. We're serving up your favorite double-decker bacon cheeseburgers and French fries for dinner tonight. Your aunt is cooking now, so it will be hot when we get home."

Luke was thinking to himself, "Hell yeah! No noodles for me tonight! I'm getting these hot Cheetos too!"

After walking through the store to retrieve his items, Bryan was politely smiling as he walked up to the counter, then said, "Hello, Bah...Bone…Kesha?" That mean, multicolored weave-wearing, cashier, scrolling on her phone, popping her gum, and talking on her AirPods said, "Hold on, girl. I got another customer…" She looked him in the eyes before rolling them and said, "IT'S BON-KWEE-SHAH! BONQUESHA! GET IT RIGHT! DON'T PLAY WIT ME! Is that all you want?... Little boy…put that on the counter so I can ring it up. I ain't got all day." After aggressively swiping the items, she said, "It's $221.89, and you can't use no EBT for that stuff either."

Looking very confused, Luke said, "Uncle B, why does that cost so much, and why did you buy those boxes that say D-N-A on them?"

"It's a very long story. We are going to talk about it in the morning." Bryan said. Luke can't believe what just happened to him. His day went from bad to good! Luke had no consequences and a snack for later. He feels like a winner! When he got home, Luke hugged his aunt and thanked her for cooking his favorite meal. After eating, Luke picks up another book and reads himself to sleep.

Did you know: *A recent study by Grethel et al. performed a* qualitative study *of 27 NPEs (Not Parent Expected). In their study, NPEs often reported a profound sense of grief and loss and an unstable sense of who they were in their family context. They reported feelings of* shock*, denial, anger, fear, confusion, isolation, extreme emotional responses, and bodily* sensations *such as feeling frozen, dazed, and dysregulated. Though the situation is of no fault of their own, many felt the discovery brought about* shame *and a desire for secrecy. Those who chose to reveal their findings often experienced their difficulties were invalidated by friends and family (*Grethel et al., 2022*).*

General Discussion:

1. Did the adults react to conflict appropriately? If so, explain. If not, what should they have done?
2. Should any character be excused for their actions? If so, why? If not, why not?

3. Why do you think Cardy trusted Luke? As a mentor, clinician, or doctor, how do you gain trust with mentees, clients, or patients?
4. At what point in a child's life are they owed the truth about important matters? Give an example and timeline.
5. Does any character's environment determine their behavior? If so, who? How?

Questions posed by Dr. Sonya Berle, DSW, LICSW, CADAC IV, ASID

Cultural and Clinical Processing

1. If the youth need assistance, how can you best support Cardy and Luke as they find out more information about their biological parents?

2. What action steps could a school implement to explore automatic thoughts further and learned actions/reactions favoring or disfavoring a student based upon their skin color? What tools, exercises, or resources could you share to raise awareness of automatic thoughts further? Action steps for teachers and staff?

3. What strengths does Cady demonstrate in this story that aid in being a bridge between her peer

group and Luke after he insulted the peers who welcomed him to play basketball?

Public Health and Structural Thinking

1. While Luke appeared oblivious to his profoundly erroneous use of a word during the basketball game, how did he perpetuate racism in his dialogue with the teachers later, and recounting his recollections of hearing the word? Does Luke appear to minimize his actions or take accountability?

2. What role does racism, towards nonwhite as compared to white students, do you see or read about in your studies, communities, and lived experiences?

3. What role did racism play in Bryan and Jasmine's (Cardy's biological parents) relationship?

A Long Weekend

Chapter 1: The Last Supper

It's Friday! All the students met in the morning at the breakfast tables in the cafeteria. They relive yesterday's events and laugh at each other about it. They start gathering all the leftovers from breakfast and plan to do the same at lunch. They know the weekend is long and they don't have food at home, only noodles. Luke goes around apologizing to all the black students he offended the day before. Luke starts explaining that he wants friends and doesn't mean to upset anyone.

"We already beat yo ass, so it's all good. Just don't do that shit again, okay?" Amari said, smiling and with his fist balled up. While laughing, he grabs Luke and hugs him, then roughs up his hair.

All the kids laughed about it, but they had other things on their minds. The weekend is here, and they all know what that means. Some of them will be hungry or not eat again until Monday when they come back to school.

"So, what's the plan?" Kyrie asked the group.

"I'll get all the milks and applesauce and fill up my bookbag," said Ernesto.

Amari yelled out, "I'll get the extra cereals and graham crackers then."

"SHHHHHHH…not so loud, bro. What about lunch, though?" Ty said with a concerned look on his face. "We got different lunch times, so what do we do?"

Cardy steps up as the leader and says, "Whatever we have today. Eat all you can, then stuff the rest in your pants like I be doing."

"That's what I do all the time, too. Just ask if you can help clean up and take everything you see. We can all just split it up on the bus when we go home." Ty said.

The volunteer reading tutor, Ms. Cindy, overhears the kids trying to find a way to get food collected to take home for themselves and their siblings. She says, "Hey… do you kids like church?

"I ain't never been? Is it fun?" Cardy said.

"Oh yes! We have church on Saturday and Sunday. We play games and have a cookout with hot dogs and burgers on both days. Y'all should come. Do all y'all live around here?

"We all take the same bus home. We live in the apartments down the street." Cardy said.

"You think your mom or dad will let you and your brother come this weekend?" Ms. Cindy asked, looking at Luke and Cardy.

"I ain't got no brother. It's just me." Cardy said.

Ms. Cindy replied, "Oh, I'm sorry, I didn't know. I thought you and he were brother and sister. Y'all look alike in those glasses."

Luke and Cardy looked at each other in shock, while the other kids pointed and laughed.

"Okay. Well, I'll follow the bus to your apartments and let your parents know that the church bus will be picking up kids at 11 am tomorrow and Sunday. Don't be late or you'll miss the bus."

"I ain't going to be late. Never! Thank you! We love you, Ms. Cindy." Cardy said, as all the students gathered around her and hugged Ms. Cindy.

Smiling with tears in her eyes from happiness, Ms. Cindy says, "Bless your little hearts. I'll see you all tomorrow. And here…take these bags. Don't stuff that food in your pants. Miss Cindy will hold on to all the food for you and bring it to you after school."

The students are so happy! They have the biggest smiles on their faces. Some are very excited, but some are still sad.

Maritza, while sinking into her chair, said, "My momma don't let me do nothing. I have to stay home and babysit while she be gone all day and night. My brother, my sister, and me be hungry! But if I leave, I'll get in trouble. Can one of y'all help me and get some food for me too?"

Cardy reached out and hugged Maritza, then said, "I know, girl. Ms. Elizabeth, don't play! She be yelling at you in Spanish all the time. Don't cry though… We got you! We are all friends, and friends help each other. Whatever we get from the school and church, we'll come by and knock on your door and leave it for y'all." Cardy reached out and helped wipe her face of tears, then continued saying, "I know, girl. It's gonna be a long weekend!"

Chapter 2: Plan A

School is finally out, and all the kids are home playing outside. Maritza has been thinking about how she is going to feed her siblings all day long. She has a 7-month-old and a 3-year-old at home with her every day. She always babysits because her mother says she has to go to work. Maritza has to make bottles, change the baby's diapers, and constantly follow the 3-year-old around to make sure he is safe. Maritza's friends are always outside playing while she stares out the window and talks with them when they stop by. Her mom has very strict rules about opening the door. "Don't ever open the door for anyone but me! If you do, I'll beat yo ass!" Maritza hears her mom's voice in her head every day when she considers letting a few friends in to use the bathroom or get water.

"Hey Maritza!!" Someone yells from outside. She comes to the window, and it's Korbyn.

With her head poking through broken and bent blinds, she replies, "What boy?"

"I need to use it. My mom said not to come in and out, or I'll have to stay in. Plus, I'm thirsty af! Can you give me some water in a cup or a water bottle?"

Maritza responds, "Hell naw…You ain't getting me in trouble. My mom will beat me down if I open this door for y'all… Anyway… You a boy! Go pee on that tree over there or behind the dumpster."

"You right… But I'm still thirsty." Korbyn reluctantly replied.

"Me too, bro!" Kyrie yelled.

Korbyn looked around and yelled out like he had discovered an ancient artifact. "Hey!! It's a water hose over there. Let's just use that to get a drink."

"Hell nah! Come on, let's go to the gas station and get something to drink." Kyrie says.

"But I ain't got no money," Korbyn said as he pulled lint and a half-eaten fruit snack out of his pockets. He is standing there with his pants pockets turned inside out, looking like rabbit ears.

Kyrie smiled with a wicked grin and said, "Me either, but I got this knife, and I know how to get drinks without getting caught."

Maritza says, "Y'all better not go over there stealing from them. If you get caught, you'll be going to the juvenile!"

"Shut up, girl, you don't know what you talkin' bout. I do this all the time, but I need a partner to make it work." Kyrie yelled back toward the window. "Let's go!"

Chapter 3: The Heist

The boys began walking to the gas station. During the brief three-block journey, they pick up some rocks to see who can throw the farthest. They discuss the scam and the need to play their roles to perfection. Korbyn was looking and acting scared. He was a little skeptical of the plan, but didn't want to look weak, so he went along.

Kyrie says, "Nigga, all you gotta do is grab some gum and ask him how much for a lottery ticket for your momma… and I'll be grabbing the two drinks and run out of the store. Damn…stop being sus!"

While at the crosswalk, Korbyn sat and shook his head back and forth, as if he was saying no, then finally agreed as they ran across the busy street to the gas station.

Kyrie walks in first with confidence and goes to the back refrigerators to get the drinks. Korbyn comes in next, looking very nervous. As he grabs some chips and gum, he says, "Hey, excuse me, sir. How much for one of them lotto tickets? It's for my mom."

The cashier calmly turns around and grabs a few different tickets to show Korbyn. "Which ones are you talking about?" the cashier said in a very deep voice. "I can't sell them to you, though. Tell your momma $1, $5, or $10. The Mega Millions is $734 million this week!"

All the while, Kyrie had the drinks and was walking toward the door. The cashier stated, "Hey, boy! I see you. Bring that up here and pay for it." Kyrie sprints out of the door like the Olympian, Usain

Bolt, in the 100m dash! He was gone! All you could hear was screeching tires, horns, and brakes from cars trying to avoid hitting him. The cashier reaches under the counter and pulls out a big black gun!

"That little bastard! I'm going to get him next time. You know him, don't you?" Korbyn was scared like he was at a haunted house on Halloween. He saw that gun, froze in his tracks, and then a little bit of pee ran down his leg. "You scared, boy? You crying? I'll give you something to cry about if you don't tell me who that boy was and where he lives."

Korbyn looked at the door with brief ambition, but didn't think he would make it, so he complied. "Ok, ok, ok… just don't shoot me, bro. We was just thirsty."

An old rusty bell hangs from a string on the door. "*BING*" is the sound it makes when someone opens the door. Upon hearing this, the cashier, Muhammed, looked toward the door and saw a customer. It's Tyler Baskins. Everybody calls him T-Bone. He's the neighborhood policeman. He walks in and says, "What's up, Muhammed! What you doing with that gun out?"

Staring in the eyes of Korbyn, he replied, "Getting ready to pop one of these bastards for stealing."

T-bone said, "Man, what they get?"

"Just some sodas and candy. But I'm tired of these fools stealing from me. It's the 3rd time this week!" Muhammed said angrily.

T-bone was holding his right hand on his gun holster and said, "Nigga you trippin, put that gun away before I take yo ass in..." Then he looked at Korbyn and said, "Hey! Ain't you Autumn's son?"

"Who?" said Muhammad.

T-bone replied, "The chick that be selling the dinners, doing hair, and babysitting out the same house!" They both laughed and looked at the boy like "oh yeah… who yo daddy boy?"

"My daddy name John Dough," Korbyn said with a shaky voice.

The two men exchanged a skeptical glance. T-bone whispered to Muhammed, "That's Butterball son for real." Then he said, "Boy! When you go home, make sure you ask your momma who Carlos Evans is."

"Ok… can I go now?" Korbyn replied. All the while, he was bouncing up and down trying to hold the rest of his pee.

Muhammed yelled out, “Hell naw. Who was that boy? What’s his name?

Korbyn said, “That's Kyrie. He’s my friend. We just wanted something to drink because we was thirsty and can’t go home yet.”

Muhammed spoke calmly and with empathy. He said, “Next time, just come here and ask. I’ll give you some work to do. You and your friend can get a sandwich and a drink every day.”

Chapter 4: Judas

T-bone directed Korbyn by the shoulder and pointed toward the police car, saying, “Get in my car, boy, I’m taking you home to talk to your mom, and you're gonna show me where Kyrie lives.”

T-bone tries talking to Korbyn on the way home. But he is overshadowed by the radio, which is requesting backup for a robbery down the street. “You lucky I showed up when I did. Me and your momma go way back to grammar school. We went to church and high school together, too, and I’m sure you already know better.” Korbyn just kept looking out the window, thinking of the lie he was going to tell when he got home.

As soon as the police car turned the corner, Korbyn

saw a lot of his friends standing outside, so he tried to duck down. "Don't act scared now!" T-bone said.

Korbyn replied, "Please don't pull up. They gonna think I'm a snitch."

T-bone laughed and said, "You are! Now get out the car and show me which house."

Korbyn, now an informant, takes the police to Kyries' house, which is next door to Maritza. Upon getting out of the car, T-bone noticed the apartment next door was loud with screams from a hungry baby. "Yo, Korbyn. Who lives here?" T-bone said, pointing at the apartment door.

T-Bone heard screams from a baby, so he banged on the door with the patented police knock, *KNOCK! KNOCK! KNOCK!* "POLICE! OPEN UP!"

"That's my other friend, Maritza. She ain't allowed to open the door until her momma come home." Korbyn whispered to the policeman.

"Who is her momma? That Mexican lady, Elizabeth?" T-bone inquired.

"Yeah, but I think they from Puerto Rico or Guatemala." Korbyn corrected him.

"Shut up, boy! Same thing... She works over at the hotel, cleaning the rooms." T-bone said while using his flashlight to look through the windows. "Well, ain't no signs of a struggle, so maybe I'll just go to the office and see if the rent lady will let me in to check. I ain't gonna call it in. But you stay right here until I get back, and don't move. Remember, I know your momma and where you live."

As T-bone walks around the corner to get to the leasing office, Maritza peeks out and says, "Is he gone?"

"Yeah, but he's coming right back," Korbyn said.

"Why you bring him over here? You know I'm going to get beat if my momma finds out… Man, you a snitch!" Maritza said, looking desperate with tears in her eyes, all while she was holding the baby on her hip.

"I didn't! I didn't! I swear!" Korbyn pleaded, then tried to explain what happened.

"Shut up, boy! We ain't friends no more!" Maritza said as she slammed the window closed.

Chapter 5: Foster Care

Finally, T-bone was back with the apartment manager and the key to get in. He sees Korbyn sitting in the same spot with his head down, looking sadder than before. The apartment had become eerily quiet since he left. KNOCK! KNOCK! KNOCK! T-bone banged on the door with the side of his fist. Then told the apartment manager, "Open it."

T-bone draws his weapon and proceeds into the apartment. He turns to see Maritza holding her sister and brother, who are watching TV. He says, "I heard a lot of screaming earlier. Are y'all okay?"

"Yes, sir. I ran out of milk earlier, but I found one in my backpack from school, so we're okay." Maritza said.

T-bone's eyes watered, so he turned and walked to his car to pull himself together. He gathered his lunch and the extra water his wife had packed for him, then brought everything into the house for the kids. "Y'all want this chicken and stuff? My wife made it for me, but I've got extra."

Maritza lit up with happiness, but still shy and reserved, said, "Thank you, police. We are hungry, and my mom won't be home until later. Can we eat it now?"

T-bone walked over dirty clothes and toys to get to the kitchen. "I'll just put it in the microwave real quick for y'all."

"That's okay. Our microwave only works sometimes, so we can just eat it like that." Maritza replied as she went to get one of the three plates from the cabinet.

"Okay, cool. I'll just leave it here. What time does your mom come home?" T-Bone said.

"When it's dark. We are usually sleeping by then." Maritza said.

Then the apartment manager, Ms. Alexandria, said, "I'm calling the Department of Child Services. These children have no business staying by themselves in these conditions. I know a lady who will come out today and take these kids to a safer place. Do you have your mom's phone number? Can you call her?"

While vacuuming a room, Elizabeth gets an alarming call from Ms. Alexandria, and in a panic, leaves her job and rushes home to find her door locked and her children gone! She came home as fast as she could, but it was too late. They have taken the children into custody and put in an order for emergency foster care. Elizabeth is losing her mind! She drops to her knees, praying frantically in Spanish. She wants her children back! She doesn't know what to do. Her English is not the best, and she needs help. She drives around the corner to the church to find Mr. Gomez.

Ms. Elizabeth parked halfway on the sidewalk and left the car running. She runs into the church in a panic and frantically says, "Señor David, por favor ayúdeme la policía se ha llevado a mis hijos." (Mr. David, please help me. The police have taken my kids.)

Mr. David Gomez is a native of Mexico but has been a U.S. citizen since he was 10. He is a former Navy SEAL and a former police officer. Now, he's a youth pastor and behavior specialist at the school with his wife. He has lots of connections in law enforcement and the church. His church has created an emergency care house for youth and families. After calming Mom down, he makes a few calls to find out what is really happening with the family.

Once Mr. David got to the root of the problem, he let Elizabeth know that they could help by keeping the children until the DCS investigation was over.

So, the police agreed to bring the children to the church and allow them to stay under Mr. David's supervision. Elizabeth was crying tears of joy but knew she had lost her job for leaving without permission. She explains to Mr. David how all this happened. He calmly translates this to Ms. Cindy, who is still there cleaning up for the Saturday youth church service. Ms. Cindy sits down by Elizabeth and prays for her, then says, "Tell her I will be putting her family on the list to receive food and clothing vouchers. She can also start cleaning our church and the event building next week while the kids are in school. That way, she can be home when the kids get out of school."

Mr. David says a whole lot in Spanish: "Pondré a su familia en la lista para recibir vales de comida y ropa. También podrá empezar a limpiar nuestra iglesia y el lugar de eventos la próxima semana mientras los niños están en la escuela. Así podrá estar en casa cuando los niños salgan de la escuela." ("I will put your family on the list to receive food and clothing vouchers. You can also start cleaning our church and event space next week while the children are at school. That way, you can be home when the children get out of school.") It seemed like he talked for like 5 minutes! Mom got up and hugged Ms. Cindy like she was a big teddy bear on

Christmas day and said, "¡Gracias!"

Chapter 6: Homeless

All the boys are up all night, on their phones, playing ROBLOX and voice chatting through the game. They talk about what happened today, and Kyrie tells them he's going to stab Korbyn for snitching. "That punk snitched on me today! When I see him, I'm going to stab him in his throat and stomach! I hate him now." The other boys are silent. They can't believe what Kyrie just said, and now they are scared to say anything.

Kyrie is a loner and always home alone. No one knows where he really lives or who he lives with. He goes from house to house, staying with his uncles, aunties, grandmother, cousin, and others. He spends the night or weekend with them so he can eat and sleep without roaches and mice around him. He doesn't know where his father is, and he only sees his mother a couple of times a week. He heard that his dad had gotten married and was living in another town about an hour away, but his dad never came to see him.

Kyrie hears about his dad coming to town and sometimes even sees him driving around with people he doesn't know. As Kyrie was walking, he saw his dad parked at a lady's house and ran up to him. "Hey, Dad! What you up to? I ain't seen you in a long time." He recalls reaching out to hug his dad, and his dad said, "Hey, son! I ain't got no money for you, so don't ask… Look here… I'm hanging out right now. I'll stop by and pick you up on my way home."

Kyrie sprinted home as fast as he could, and this time his mom was home. "Mom! Mom! I just saw Dad. He said he was coming to get me in a few minutes, so I have to pack my stuff real quick."

His mom looked at him, exhausted from work and with a heavy heart, said, "Son, you can take your time. It's already pretty late. Maybe he meant he would come tomorrow."

"No way, Mom. I saw him. He said he's coming, so I'm getting ready now." Kyrie remembers wanting to hang out with his dad so badly that he rushed to his room and packed whatever clothes he could find. He even got some stuff out of the dirty clothes pile and put it in his backpack. After packing his clothes, he sat by the door and stared out the window for hours. Every car that came down the street, he stood up and grabbed his backpack. They were all false alarms. Kyrie eventually fell asleep on the floor, still wearing his backpack. When he woke up, he was a new person. Kyrie was constantly depressed and angry. He told himself, "I ain't never believing him again. I don't need nobody!"

Every time he is outside, someone comes up and asks, "Is your daddy John Dough?" When he answers yes, they share a story about how cool he was and how they used to party and run the streets together. Adversely, when he is at any of his family members' homes, his cousins would tease him and say, "You know your daddy ain't shit! My momma said he was on drugs, and he don't want you or your momma!" Kyrie always held back his tears and just made up stories about seeing his father, just to get them to stop.

Loyalty is everything to Kyrie. If you're his friend, he will do anything for you and watch your back. That's what made him so angry with Korbyn. He tried to steal so that both of them would have a drink and felt like Korbyn brought the police to find him and get him locked up. Kyrie has always felt abandoned, but he has his crew, Amari and Ty. They help sneak him in at night to sleep and give him clothes and food when they have it. They are best friends. Kyrie is a tough kid who never backs down from the bigger kids. He will fight anyone and use weapons to win. He won't let anything happen to Ty and Amari if bigger kids are trying to bully them.

Chapter 7: Homecoming

Meanwhile, it's dark, and all the police cars are gone. Kyrie feels like it's safe to go back to his apartment complex. He walks through different groups of people to get through the neighborhood: a motorcycle crew wearing black leather, older kids on dirt bikes, packs of guys holding the leashes of the scarred-up pit bulls, loud talking women smoking cigarettes, and men with loud music playing out of the cars with the big shiny wheels on them. There are other people drinking beers, vaping, smoking little brown cigars, and some are shooting dice on the ground with lots of dollar bills scattered around. There are also different groups of girls walking from one crew of men to another, as if they are selling something. They either wear very tight clothes or wear almost nothing at all. They all have long eyelashes and lots of makeup on their faces. Kyrie knows to be careful and keep his head down when he walks through the hood at night. One of the dirt bike boys yelled out, "Who is that little nigga?"

There is a big boss of the guys wearing red clothes, bandanas, and du-rags. His name is Big Cheese.

While sitting on the hood of his long red convertible Cadillac, he had two women draped over him, rubbing his shoulders and head. There were also three muscular, gun-toting, shirtless, tattooed guys wearing sunglasses, looking out for him. They paced around his area, screening anyone who came within range of him. Big Cheese was holding up a big chrome gun in his right hand, his left hand at his side with a bankroll of cash, held together by dirty rubber bands. With glossy red eyes and a serious look on his face, he yelled out, "Let that boy pass every time. Better not nobody mess with him, or they gotta deal with me! That boy is gonna be something one day. Y'all watch what I tell you." As they watch Kyrie disappear into the darkness of the concrete jungle.

Once he's out of sight of the people, he jogs straight to Amari's window and knocks lightly. Amari looked over and excitedly said, "Kyrie!! Climb in, bro. I'm glad you okay."

Kyrie told Amari what happened and that he just wanted to eat something. "Do y'all got some food? I'm starving, bro." Amari sneaks to the kitchen and makes Kyrie a bowl of noodles, but when he gets back to his room, Kyrie is asleep on the floor.

Chapter 8: Saturday

"Get up, man. It's a rag and some clothes in the bathroom. Hurry up and get ready. We gotta be outside in 10 minutes to catch the church bus." Amari said to Kyrie.

"Ok, cool. Thanks for letting me stay. I was super tired… I'm still getting Korbyn today!" Kyrie said, after getting up from the floor and heading to the bathroom.

When he returned, Amari talked to him about what would happen if he stabbed Korbyn. "Bro! If you stab him, you're going to jail, and we won't see you again. It ain't that deep. We all talked to him yesterday, and he said that the guy in the gas station pulled a gun on him and was going to shoot him if he didn't tell."

While Kyrie was putting Amari's favorite shirt over his head, he stopped and said, "For real? Dang. I didn't know that. I didn't mean for this to happen. I just wanted to get us a drink real quick. I ain't finna hurt him. Just tell him, we cool, and I'll see him at the church."

"Bet! I'm calling him now." Amari reaches for his phone and facetimes Korbyn. "Bro! Kyrie ain't mad at you no more. He wanna to talk real quick."

Kyrie was shaking his head no, but Amari handed him the phone. "What's up, man? You good? I ain't mad at you, bro."

Korbyn said, "Yeah, man, I'm sorry about yesterday, but I was scared and didn't know what to do. That dude had a big black gun and made me pee on myself…" They both laughed out loud, and Korbyn continued, "My momma beat me good last night, so I can't go outside and play, but I can go to church. She said I'm on punishment too."

"Ok, bet. I'll see you there." Kyrie said with a smile.

Upon arrival at the church, they all got out of the little white and blue church bus and ran to Ms. Cindy, who was waiting for them at the door. When they walked in, they saw Maritza and her siblings in new clothes, along with a large amount of food on the back table.

"Y'all kids go and eat, then we'll sit down and do some activities." Ms. Cindy said loudly.

Maritza ran over to Kyrie, hugged him, and said, "Are you okay? I heard they couldn't find you."

"Yeah, I was at Amari's house last night. I was scared to go home." Kyrie said. "But wait… y'all got on new clothes and shoes. How did you get all this stuff?"

Maritza explained to Kyrie what happened when they were looking for him. She told him how the church let them stay for the weekend, gave them food and clothes, and even gave her mom a new job so she could stay home and watch them. "I might get to start coming outside to play with y'all now. I'm so happy! Wait… you should ask Ms. Cindy and Mr. David to help you, too. They talked and prayed about you last night."

Kyrie is getting ready to cry and says, "For real? Nobody ever done that for me except my granny, a long time ago. I'll ask Ms. Cindy and Mr. David and see what they say. I hope they say yes. I'm getting tired of everyone making fun of me, and I just want to lay in a bed. I haven't done that in a long, long time."

Korbyn comes walking up very quietly and humbly, with his head down, and says, "Maritza, I'm so sorry. I didn't try to get you in trouble. But…"

Maritza stopped him and said, "I forgive you. That's what Ms. Cindy told us last night. We have to learn to forgive people. No one is perfect, and we all make mistakes… but she also said something about Moses, Joshua, Jesus, and somebody else, I can't remember all that, but we got to eat after we listened to her… See my new clothes and stuff! I'm happy everything happened. Now give me a hug!" As she reached out for Korbyn, he started crying, saying I'm sorry, y'all. Kyrie joined in the hug. When everyone saw them hugging, they ran to them and surrounded them with the biggest group hug 15 kids could have.

Did you know: *"Hunger negatively affects children during the school day by causing poor academic performance, behavioral problems, and health issues. These children have difficulty concentrating, which can lead to lower grades, increased absenteeism, and a higher likelihood of repeating a grade. Hunger can also cause irritability, stress, and anxiety, which may manifest as hyperactivity, withdrawal, or aggression. Health-wise, it increases risks for conditions like anemia and can impact a child's overall growth and development."* Feedingamerica.org

General Discussion:

1. What adults were protective of children? How did they show it?
2. How do you feel when you don't have enough resources to help the children you work with? What do you do with those feelings? Do you make sacrifices for clients? If so, what kind?

3. Would any of the children be better off in foster care? Why? What is your expected outcome from reporting?
4. Describe any feelings you felt. How does your body respond to these feelings? (e.g., sweating, heart rate, tension, etc.) Explain, then identify the emotion.
5. How does your attitude, emotions, and physical state change when you are sleepy or hungry? Should your actions be excused?

Questions posed by Dr. Sonya Berle, DSW, LICSW, CADAC IV, ASID

Cultural and Clinical Processing

1. When pondering clinician and educator self-awareness and assumption making, how different do you think Ms. Alexandra's (apartment manager) interpretation of Ms. Elizabeth's family was as compared to the church pastor's interpretation of Ms. Elizabeth's intention towards her children?

2. Clinically, what role does attachment theory perhaps play in Kyrie's meaning-making system of a safe and secure world? What attachment style would you explore with him? What are his resiliency factors in his current life and community that can

mitigate stressors arising from his relationship with his father?

Public Health and Structural Thinking

1. How does your anticipation of a weekend look similar or different than the youth's interpretation of a weekend as presented in this story?

2. Did the Department of Child Services work in tandem with Ms. Elizabeth and her family? What barriers did Ms. Elizabeth have to contend with while under duress and the crisis of child removal?

3. We again see community helping each other as Ms. Cindy, the cafeteria staff member, helped children prepare food for the weekend. What other cross-connectivity occurred in this story in which adults and systems interacted to mitigate poor outcomes for youth? Can you name two?

Reflections Key:

A Next Step Read to Catalyze Clinical, Cultural, and Environmental Processing Ideas

Each section of Mr. Ahmad Kersey's book contains a story followed by three reflection and engagement parts. Part One is Story Engagement, Part Two is Cultural and Clinical Processing, and Part Three is Public Health and Structural Thinking. Below, you will find a social worker's lens and some educational considerations, provided in a trauma-focused, biopsychosocial-spiritual assessment style, to read, ponder, and potentially integrate clinically with the reflection questions and action steps. You will find some underlined questions throughout this section.

Biography of the Introduction to Reflections Writer

Sonya Berle is a Doctor of Social Work and an independently clinically licensed social worker with extensive educational and experiential work in trauma and crisis. Berle's doctoral focus is on a new framework operating at a nexus to examine traumatic stressors and chronic absenteeism, the effects of environment on the student and family system, with a primary focus on Black urban middle school youth. Aspects of Hispanic youth's adverse experiences and outcomes are also presented in Berle's doctoral materials. Berle holds a trauma specialization from her clinical social work master's education and focused on the Black young adult male experience in America during her studies.

Berle is currently contracted as a Senior Triage Supervisor/Subject Matter Expert in the greater Washington, D.C., area for Military OneSource, serving soldiers and families in the United States Armed Forces. Berle had extensive on-the-ground mental health and substance use disorder clinical intervention experience partnering with youth and families in Title I schools, and clients unhoused in Indianapolis, IN, Providence, RI, and Charleston, SC. Berle trained at the National Crime Victims Research & Treatment Center at the Medical University of South Carolina. She has worked nationally with mandated and non-mandated clients in substance use disorder care, examining drivers, and creating TIP sheets and education workshops for prevention. Lastly, she holds an additional master's degree in integrative health coaching practices and a national certification in the design of residential and commercial interior spaces. Berle assesses, diagnoses, treats, and educates deeply from a social determinant of health and wellness lens, examining the catalyzing and potentiating effects of the environment on the person and/or system. She is guided by the social work values of dignity and worth of each person, trauma-informed care, positive psychology, and a strength-based lens, and is a proud daughter of a veteran. She understands that poverty and trauma do not know boundaries, and she is fueled to partner with humanity daily, instilling hope and strength; together, we got this!

Disclaimer

In the current, continually changing socio-political landscape, the populations affected by isms, poverty, and trauma, and the scope of their impact on social determinants of health, is much broader and more complex than can be provided in Dr. Berle's educational pages. However, the pages are grounded in social work core values, evidence-based practices, research, adverse experiences leading to chronic absenteeism from school, and the exhaustion youth experience from barriers, and they reference theorists and theories in the behavioral science domain. The writer has received neither compensation nor conflicts of interest with any materials or parties referenced in this work. For a complete reference list, questions, or presentation needs, don't hesitate to contact Sonya Berle, DSW, LICSW, CADAC IV, ASID Associate, at sonya@decreasestress.net.

Human Developmental Considerations for Late Elementary to Early High School

The cognitive, socio-emotional, and physiological developmental changes during these educational years are profound, dynamic, and intersect acutely with youth-reported increased awareness of traumatic exposures and toxic stress that include poverty, racism, and systemic oppression events affecting wellness and school attendance. The literature supports youth self-reports. Immediately after middle school, chronic absenteeism and school dropout rates spike, for example, and the causes are primarily environmental. When reading Mr. Kersey's stories, please attend to the golden thread of environmental exacerbations recounted and the intervention opportunities to mitigate stressors. Some theorists to consider are Dr. Urie Bronfenbrenner's Person in Environment (PIE), Dr. Kimberlee Crenshaw's Intersectionality, and Dr. Arline Geronimus Weathering Theory. From a strengths-based lens, how many potential intervention points can you find in each story?

What Can Schools Do? Belongingness is Critical to Student Success

Absenteeism, Poverty, and Barriers to School Attendance

Heidi Chang, an expert on chronic absenteeism and founder of Attendance Works, states, "My first question would be, 'Do I make sure that every kid has an adult on that campus they can talk to?'" Chang said. She said that physical and emotional safety, and a sense of belonging, are among the core conditions necessary to engage students. Chang states, "You can send out communications saying, 'We miss you,' but if a student does not feel like anybody at the school cares about them, some little note might not do a lot" (Rix, 2024, p.3).

To continue pondering belongingness for youth to mitigate absenteeism, Mendelson et al.'s trauma-informed urban eighth-grade intervention measuring absenteeism and suspension rates (Project POWER), Promoting Options for Wellness and Emotional Regulation (Mendelson et al., 2020), takes a holistic approach to multidimensional factors directly causing and contributing to chronic absenteeism in 32 Baltimore urban schools. The Center for Connecticut Education Research Collaboration utilized LEAP

(Learner Attention and Engagement Program) in 2021 to re-engage chronically absent students post-COVID. Profoundly positive attendance rate increases of 30% were observed in the Hartford district, for example, and home visits were more efficacious than telehealth. The human touch, time taken, and insight school staff gained into home environs led to increased student attendance and feelings of belonging once at school (Stemler et al., 2022). *Thematically, Weak Daze at a Public School threads the community both within the school (among peer groups) and externally, with adults helping youth when systemic barriers exist. What action steps and intervention points are taken in school? Do you notice where youth feel a sense of belongingness from adults?*

Punishment

Disparate punishment also increases the rates of grade repeats and dropouts (Chen, 2022). This action by educators and the subsequent reaction of internalizing destructive messages sent to Black youth add significant and varying absenteeism rates for Black youth. School-based infractions also demonstrate racism's effects and standards that inequitably reprimand using a skin-colored lens and hold the problem in place. Some research reveals that receiving even one out-of-school suspension increases the CA risk rate by 350% (J. E. Ford & Triplett, 2019). The Department of Education's Civil Rights Office found that Black youth are punished more harshly than their White peers for the same infractions (Chen, 2022). Nationally, Black students comprise 15% of enrolled K-12 children yet receive 38% of the exclusionary discipline (US Department of Education, 2021). How many interactions leading to infractions did you find in Mr. Kersey's stories? What thematic barriers to attending school were overtly and others covertly described in these stories?

Embarrassment

Most importantly, for all middle school youth, regardless of gender, gender identity, race, or ethnicity, do NOT call them out in front of peers. Middle school youth's developmental stage leaves them significantly vulnerable to being "called out" in front of peers and to caring what adults think, yet to shutting down quickly if they feel "not liked" by an adult. Youth are acutely aware of each other's judgments and acceptances. When they shut down, they stop showing up, too. Please consider adult-to-student interactions and who is called out during the scenarios. Also, can being called out look and feel differently to different youth? How many different ways might a student exhibit embarrassment externally? What might happen internally and to belongingness?

Being Heard

Mental health is now a national crisis, as factors of adverse childhood experiences (ACE), poverty, racism, plus COVID-19 grief, loss, and disruption, converge. Youth interviewed by Dr. Berle report anxiety, stress, and feelings of overwhelm, which decrease their ability to focus on school learning. They report that the inclusion of youth voices in exploring problem and solution spaces is not universal; middle school youth feel unheard. Alternatively, if a need is expressed, conventional funding lanes cannot address it. Teachers are experiencing burnout because they feel helpless. Do you notice instances or interactions that portray teacher or caregiver burnout in these stories? What signs, symptoms, and criteria met for burnout do you read in these stories?

Research

Using the CBPAR approach and ethnographic study, Sonya Berle collected data from 338 local stakeholders, users, and beneficiaries from December 2022 to June 2024 via self-reports, structured and unstructured in-person interviews, Zoom meetings, and anonymous qualitative and quantitative surveys. National and international expert interviews were also conducted. Iterating occurred at Indianapolis Public Schools in the same geographic locale and population as the author, Mr. Kersey, and LSC, as presented in his expert on-the-ground recounting, reflective of the Indianapolis urban environment and mirroring nationwide accounts of school-aged child and family concerns in other urban American environments. Berle's research culminates in a new framework that shifts the onus off youth and provides a thinking and intervention template for equitable access to holistic, evidence-based resources and action steps to improve the social determinants of health outcomes for youth and families. Mr. Ahmad Kersey's *Weak Daze at a Public School* brings eloquently painful voice, poignance, and the irony of perceptions and environments to life in his embodied expertise contained in this book.

Social Determinants of Health and Inequitable Starts from Childhood

Learning

A goal is to continue bringing equitable opportunity to learn, understand, and positively change and nurture the cross-connectivity of the environment, both internal and external, and its effects on all forms of human wellness and the social determinants of health. Let us give all youth a more environmentally level playing field at the outset so human brains can develop beyond the Scarcity Mindset. When humans' basic needs are not met, other brain centers cannot activate and flourish. The primitive brain is activated, and learning centers are offline (Braveman et al., 2022, p.3). Have you experienced this? Neuroscience helps us understand the chronic production of stress hormones, which affect learning, memory, emotional processing, and mental health (Appendix A). New research finds structural racism, with poverty as a primary driver, and traumatic events affect the hippocampus, prefrontal cortex development, and amygdala development; gray matter volume differences exist between Black and White children (Dumornay et al., 2023; HMS, 2021; Schauble & Lu, 2023). If kids hold traumatic stress, they cannot learn. Consequences of traumatic stressors create threat appraisal and unrest for the human mind. The brain shunts processes, reserves resources, and is in survival mode, not memory mode (Schauble & Lu, 2023). When they do not learn, they disengage."

Longevity

One measurable lifespan data category for Indianapolis urban residents. The 2015 life expectancy was 69.4, yet in neighboring Carmel, with only 3.53% Black residents (WPR, 2024), it is 83.7 years, and in the 46218-zip code with 68.1% Black residents, it is currently 68.1 years (CISF, 2023). "A baby born in South Central Indianapolis is expected to live a shorter life than a baby born in Iraq (Weathers et al., 2015, p.1)." The disparity of life expectancies occurs in other American cities, too.

Education

Educational setting for youth illuminates the ongoing burden for Black students who are 3.5 times more likely than whites to attend a chronically underfunded public school (J. Williams, 2024), denoted an "Inequality Factory" in the article's title. The higher-poverty districts are less funded, leading to equity gaps across multiple SDOH domains. Further illuminating ongoing actions, some states are reported to have funds available yet not allocated. Williams denotes them as "low effort states (J. Williams, 2024, p. 5)."

At the national level, Fiscal Year (FY) 2023-24

presents the same problem at the postsecondary level, where level funding, budget caps, and inflation are leaving fewer funds for Pell and low-income students with basic-needs financial assistance (Knox, 2024; McKibben & Huelsman, 2024). As the Vice President of Education Trust states, "The failure to increase investments in those programs is particularly damaging for Black, Latino, and Native students and students from low-income backgrounds," Augustus Mays (Knox, p.3, 2024).

Earned Income

A brief example of economic disparity is provided by the Opportunity Atlas, which reveals that Black children growing up in the urban core of Mass. Ave. earned $20,000 per year, once adults, compared to their White adult neighbors, who earned $55,000. The same is seen in Emerson Heights, where income disparity is $26,000 (Colombo, 2018). The Fair Housing in Indiana 2022 report illuminates reports of gentrification and Black loan denial rates as two to five times higher than white denial rates are reported (2018-2021), along with a 14% decline in Black homeownership across the county, with historically Black neighborhood residents experiencing significant displacement (FHCCI, 2022; Rafford, 2022).

Policy Meeting Practice Problems

Of critical importance, no matter what solution is presented, is the outcome versus intention. The McKinney-Vento Act, which protects confidentiality and provides continuity of education and activity funds for unhoused students, who are disproportionately Black (Cermak, 2018; NCHE, 2020), reminds us of the continual need to assess policy-to-practice outcomes. The subgrants deliver benefits to Title I schools (U.S. Department of Education, 2018), yet competitive grant application processes lure wealthier schools to hire grant writers. Only New Jersey received subgrant funding for all its LEAs in 2018 (NCHE, 2020). The MV fund availability and disbursement are critically important to the Indianapolis Public School Black community, where 82% of Indianapolis unhoused families with young children are Black, according to the Coalition for Homeless Intervention and Prevention (Waiss, 2022) with a 44% increase, from 2020-21 to 2023-24 in students who are experiencing homelessness across the state (Hylton, 2025). National data mirrors Indiana's trend.

What is Trauma-Informed Care and Why Does It Matter?

Trauma-informed care (TIC) is a strengths-based, evidence-based approach credited to the original work of Fallot & Harris (2001) and proven efficacious in healthcare settings, schools, and living/working space design for unhoused and race-specific populations (SAMHSA, 2022). "Becoming trauma-informed means recognizing that people have many different traumatic experiences which often intersect in their lives (National Coalition for the Homeless, 2022, p.1). Berle adheres to the trauma definition of an experience that overwhelms the system's capacity to cope. Can you discuss and describe traditional and non-traditional examples of overwhelm for a person (or system)? This holistic and person-centered understanding of trauma can help the clinician, caregiver, teacher, and adult to think of trauma with a broader scope and understand behavioral and symptomology-based responses from youth under duress. It can also help adults create mitigating and buffering environments to reduce the impact of episodic and chronic events on the system. Student externalized responses directly affect youth and families in school systems. TIC can also support the social work code of ethics principles, including each person's dignity and self-worth (Arlene Loera, 2017). This monumental shift from internal to external variables aligns with social work core values (NASW, 2019), systems theory, and person-in-environment approaches (Adams et al., 2014; Bronfenbrenner, 1986; Rosa & Tudge, 2013) as seen in TIC.

The TIC framework also addresses the complexities and is delivered with an understanding of structural racism (SAMHSA, 2021). One of the six guiding principles, Cultural, Historical, and Gender Issues, directly names racism, and the other five principles address toxic stress exposures (TICIRC, 2020).

A **Clinical Intervention Point for Diagnosed Post-Traumatic Stress Disorder**

From a positive psychology perspective and in searching for intervention points, we know supporting persons, interventions, and environments in the youth's life mitigate the impact of traumatic events and allow for opportunities for post-traumatic growth. One clinical intervention, for example, trauma-focused cognitive behavioral therapy (TFCBT), is a best-practice intervention for children and families. Its structured, methodological process provides, at the outset, a myriad of insight-building and coping skills that both buffer and strengthen the youth's system and capacity to cope.

TF-CBT is a gold standard treatment for ages three to eighteen (de Arellano, 2020; MUSC, 2017) while providing an opportunity for culturally adapting trauma narratives (Woods-Jaeger et al., 2017), a Spanish as first language TF-CBT (MUSC, 2020), and three pillars of a culturally adapted TF-CBT for Black teens that validates risk factors of racial stress and trauma while recognizing racial socialization's buffering effects (Metzger, 2020).

Some Diagnostic Considerations

1. Diagnosis-in both mental health and substance use diagnosis, please triage safety first and then move to the least restrictive and least stigmatizing labels for youth.

2. During assessments and diagnosis, please always include rule-outs and rationale. While this might take more time, in our ever-pressed clinical days and deadlines, it can provide important insight for future considerations as clinical teams and collaterals get to know the client better and as the client begins to build comfort, insight, and communication skills with adults. Client articulation of symptomatology causing the most distress, drivers of behaviors and symptoms, environmental history, and other elements not initially discussed at intake may evolve over time and significantly

change the diagnostic landscape.

3. Please continuously practice self-awareness skills and ask open-ended questions to glean the youth's perception, value system, cultural considerations, and self-reported areas of distress. Their idea of crisis and cause can differ significantly from the clinician's or caregiver's perception. As we keep reminding ourselves, it is the age when youth do not want to be "told" what to do, and it is a fragile transition time for caregivers parenting a rising teen and a rising adult who is no longer a child. Please provide feelings validation at the onset.

ABOUT THE AUTHOR

Ahmad Kersey is a behavioral health professional, educator, and entrepreneur with more than 25 years of experience serving youth and families in urban communities. He is the Founder and President of ARK Health & Social Services, a comprehensive family support agency in Indiana specializing in family preservation, behavioral health services, literacy development, and home-based therapeutic care.

Throughout his career, Ahmad has worked within schools, healthcare systems, and court-involved settings, supporting children and families facing trauma, poverty, and systemic barriers. His work focuses on the intersection of mental health, literacy, equity, and social determinants of health. He has led programs supporting FSSA, DMHA, and Department of Child Services (DCS) families, developed youth literacy initiatives, and created stabilization programs designed to strengthen family structure and long-term outcomes.

Ahmad holds a Bachelor of General Studies from Ball State University with minors in Communication Studies and Business

Administration. He is certified in mental health services, Personal Services Agency License, Wraparound Habilitation and Respite Provider; Certified Nurturing Parenting Program Facilitator; and Suicide Interventionist Certification (CAMS-care). His mission is to create practical, culturally responsive solutions that improve behavioral health outcomes and empower underserved communities.

Let's work together! If there are any projects to help fight the Social Determinants of Health, please leave your contact info on:

www.arkhealthsocial.com

Letter From the Author

In my 25 years of working with students, I have consistently observed that many behavioral challenges stem from students' struggles with reading and comprehending instructions. When children find it difficult to understand assignments, frustration and disengagement often follow. This frustration can build over time, leading to disruptive behaviors in the classroom and, in some cases, escalating to more serious or even dangerous actions as students' progress toward high school. For example, when a student cannot keep up with reading expectations, they may act out to divert attention from their academic difficulties or avoid tasks that make them feel inadequate. Supporting this, a 2020 study found that students with lower reading proficiency were more likely to exhibit disciplinary issues in middle and high school. These patterns highlight the critical need to address literacy early to help prevent the escalation of behavioral problems as reading levels decline with age.

Once I asked about moving a highly intelligent student to more advanced class, an anonymous public-school teacher replied, "We've been told to bring these types of kids back to the pack."

Since 54% of Americans read at a 6th-grade level, this literature is intentionally crafted for readers with 4th- to 6th-grade reading abilities. This approach is designed to make the story welcoming and accessible, allowing the entire family—regardless of age or reading skill—to share in the experience and enjoy the story together. It also ensures that everyone can participate fully, fostering family engagement and connection. The aim is to highlight the everyday world of 4th-grade students growing up in public schools across America. People often overlook how advanced these children are in areas such as problem-solving, creativity, and social skills. Even if their reading abilities don't match their grade level, they demonstrate remarkable talents and abilities in ways that go far beyond academics.

I created this book to recognize the struggles of all the children in poverty all around America. When I was growing up, I wasn't always poor. I started my consciousness in my grandparents' home, living with my mom, Granny, Grampa, and my uncles, Reggie and Karl. I had everything a kid could want. I lived in a mansion! But looking back, the house is surprisingly only 2100 square feet! I was only 2 feet tall, so everything seemed larger than life. We had 20-foot vaulted ceilings, two pear trees in the backyard, a grape vine, collard greens growing under the back porch, and a huge pine tree in the front yard, which I thought was a Christmas tree during the winter months.

I was an only child in a house with what I thought were five adults. In actuality, it was only 2 adults, Mary and Gene Kersey, and 4 children. My uncles were 18 and 15, and my mother was 17. Sounds like a breeze, right? Wrong!! At times, I was the subject of discussion and scrutiny, unable to defend myself, speak my mind, or even escape my problems. In fact, I spent most days alone in the comfort of my imagination. I dreamed of being Roger Staughbach, Tony Dorsett, Dr. J, or Mario Andretti while playing with my football or Hot Wheels cars on the orange racetracks. Those tracks doubled as a tool for beating children in my neighborhood during the late 1970s and early 1980s.

One Christmas, I finally got the Dallas Cowboys helmet and the black electric-car racetrack you had to put together. I started with the circle track, but eventually upgraded to the F1 circuit track, only for my cousin Carlos to step on it and break it! Once my uncles moved out, I had the entire upstairs to myself. I had a bedroom, bathroom, and living room, all filled with toys. My uncles decorated the walls with Sports Illustrated magazine covers featuring Muhammad Ali, the Dallas Cowboys, Pittsburgh Steelers, Reggie Jackson in the Oakland A's uniform, Mean Joe Greene, Ed "Too Tall" Jones, Bruce Jenner from the Wheaties box, Roberto Clemente, Dr. J, and other athletes I was too young to know. These were all pictures that my uncles left behind to help my imagination.

At night, I would be terrified to go up the stairs by myself. The only light switch was at the top of the stairs, and I had to stand on my tiptoes to reach it. It was a push-button light that had to be pressed in to come on, which took more strength than a 4-year-old could handle. I would get close to the top and see those eyes staring at me. There were 2 square windows in the kitchen area of my upstairs apartment; they stayed lit up at night from the streetlight on the corner. I was always horrified!! I remember trying to turn on the light and tumbling down the stairs like a rag doll, finally stopping to cry for my momma, then slipping down the last five stairs, only to get a laugh from the entire family. I had those zip-up pajamas with feet that had no grip! I didn't know any other life.

During the holidays, there was love and family. My grampa would take me with him to cut down a Christmas tree every year. I would shoot the moon from a .410 rifle on New Year's and always had a cake for my birthday. There were pear and peach preserves in Ball jars, stacked up to the ceiling in the kitchen. The house was always immaculate, and dinner was at 6 pm sharp every night, no exception. I could ride my bike in the street with the other kids. Everyone on the block was like family. Anyway, those days soon passed. My mom moved out and took me with her. This experience sucked! I was now a poor kid. I lived in subpar conditions, and we moved a lot. Everywhere I lived, there were either roaches or mice, sometimes both. We even had a bat in the house a few times. I hated my new life. Back then, food stamps were paper. I might find one now and again, go to the "Milk House" for candy, and keep the 90 cents for my piggy bank.

House parties were a thing back then in the late 1970s (and continued through to the 1990s). When it was party time, I always had to go to bed. I couldn't sleep through all that noise. Sometimes, I'd hang out with other random kids whose parents came over to party with my mom and her boyfriend. He had a son, who became my new brother. John-John and I would wake up early while my mom and his dad were sleeping, pretending to be grown-ups and doing what we heard them doing last night. We would take the cigarette butts and put them in our mouths like we were smoking. We took sips from the cups left over with brown liquid in them, not knowing we were tasting Seagram's Seven and Coke until one of us tried to swallow and spit it out. We put the roach clips with feathers (for smoking the marijuana joints) on our ears, like Mr. T earrings, and all this before anyone woke up to bother us.

As I got older, my experience changed, but it didn't improve significantly. I was still poor, just like most of my friends. Some were worse off than I was, but a few were better off. I always had free lunch and a key around my neck to get into the house after school. There was not much supervision during the 1980s. Every night the news would say, "Its 10pm. Parents, do you know where your children are?" Anyway, I'm saying all this to show that I know what it's like to be a poor kid and not be able to do anything about it.

I wrote this from the vantage point of a poor kid from the 1970s all the way to today, the 2020s. The same traumas are inflicted on kids, but they manifest differently. These fictional stories are very real! I was a fly on the wall for some, and I experienced some of these stories myself. During the time I wrote this book, I've had 25 years of experience working with youth and families in mental/behavioral health settings, schools, the community, and facilities. I'm dedicating this to all the "rejected, ghetto, trailer trash, hillbilly, redneck, poor kids" that no one cares about. I see you! I see your struggles! I see your pain! It will not last forever! You must endure your struggles to tell your story one day. I'm rooting for you to win. Remember this: everything you go through will not make sense at the time, but you will be able to use it as fuel in the future. Let the fuel propel you to greatness and success, whatever that means to you. Don't give up!

Your friend,

Mr. Ahmad.

The Brain Dump.

Express your thoughts here:

www.ingramcontent.com/pod-product-compliance
Lightning Source LLC
LaVergne TN
LVHW090519110826
845146LV00003B/914